EVEREST
BOOK THREE
THE SUMMIT

GORDON KORMAN

EVEREST

BOOK THREE
THE SUMMIT

SCHOLASTIC INC.
New York Toronto London Auckland
Sydney Mexico City New Delhi Hong Kong

For Daisy Samantha Korman
My Summit

No part of this publication may be reproduced, stored in a retrieval system, or transmitted in any form or by any means, electronic, mechanical, photocopying, recording, or otherwise, without written permission of the publisher. For information regarding permission, write to Scholastic Inc., Attention: Permissions Department, 557 Broadway, New York, NY 10012.

ISBN 978-0-545-39234-1

Copyright © 2002 by Gordon Korman. All rights reserved. Published by Scholastic Inc. SCHOLASTIC and associated logos are trademarks and/or registered trademarks of Scholastic Inc.

12 11 10 9 8 7 6 5 4 3 2 1   12 13 14 15 16 17/0

Printed in the U.S.A.   40

This edition first printing, March 2012

PROLOGUE

The wind pounced on them above twenty-five thousand feet.

As the youngest expedition in Everest history scrambled up the Geneva Spur, the onslaught began — overpowering, unpredictable gusts that threatened to pluck the climbers off the mountain and hurl them into space.

Amazingly, this was nothing new to them. This was the second time the team had stood atop the Spur, a mammoth club of decaying black rock in the infamous Death Zone high on Everest. Their last summit bid had been scuttled when they'd been called away to perform a daring high-altitude rescue. For two very long weeks, the SummitQuest climbers had waited at Base Camp, begging fate for the weather to offer a second chance at the peak.

Now they had it. And, as team leader Cap Cicero put it, "We're not going to let a little breeze get in our way."

Clad in full-body wind suits, oxygen masks, and goggles, the SummitQuest mountaineers looked like something out of a science fiction movie. This was fitting, since the pinnacle of the world was as inhospitable a place as any alien planet.

Bent double into the teeth of the gale, they slogged on, gasping bottled oxygen, moving slowly, but always moving. At extreme altitude, the mere effort of putting one foot in front of the other is the equivalent of pushing a boulder up a steep hill. It takes massive reserves of strength and will. And it takes the ability to fight through pain.

A sudden howling blast drove thirteen-year-old Dominic Alexis back a step. Cicero reached out a hand to steady his youngest and smallest alpinist. Then he guided the boy into line behind him in an effort to shelter him from the worst of the fierce wind.

Cicero's confident stance belied an inner concern: *If the blow's this bad here, it's bound to be murderous higher up.*

Normally, conditions like this would have sent a team back to Base Camp to wait for better weather. But it was the twenty-first of May, very late in the climbing season. Any day, Everest's summer monsoon could begin, effectively shutting down the mountain. They climbed now because they could not be sure they would get another chance.

The team leader had no way of knowing that summer would come late that year. Nor could he have foreseen that, before Everest slipped into the monsoon, it would claim the life of one of his young climbers.

CHAPTER ONE

Camp Four was a handful of tents on the South Col, the desolate, wind-scoured valley between the titanic peaks of Everest and Lhotse. At twenty-six thousand feet, it was more than a mile higher than Mount McKinley, the loftiest pinnacle in North America, and two miles higher than any point in the lower forty-eight states.

True to Cicero's expectations, conditions were appalling on the Col. The air temperature was $-17°$ F, made bone-cracking by a wind that, at sea level, would have been considered a Category 2 hurricane.

"We can't climb in this!" complained Perry Noonan, shouting to be heard over the howling gale. "It's going to be a million below zero at the summit!"

"It could die down in an hour," soothed Lenny "Sneezy" Tkakzuk, panning the bleak wasteland of rock and ice with his camera. It was Sneezy's job to document their adventures on videotape. The footage would be E-mailed via satellite phone to their sponsor, Summit Athletic Corporation, for release on the Internet.

"Or it could stay like this for two weeks!" Perry countered.

"It's not rocket science," put in Babu Pemba, the head Sherpa guide, or Sirdar. "If it eases up, we climb. If it doesn't, we turn around."

"I'm not going down," announced Tilt Crowley defiantly. "This is our last chance. I don't care about the rest of you guys. *I'm* going to the summit."

Cicero glared at him. "You'll go where I tell you to, Crowley. Now let's all try to get some rest. Standing here freezing isn't going to change the weather."

It was just before three P.M. The summit bid was to begin in nine hours — an all-night marathon climb, returning before dark the next day.

If everything goes as planned, Perry reminded himself. The problem was that in the Death Zone nothing ever went as planned.

In the teen climbers' tent, Tilt, Perry, Dominic, and their fourth teammate, Samantha Moon, the only girl, snacked on Summit Energy Bars and waited for the stove to melt ice. At this altitude, fire burned at such a low temperature that a simple cup of instant soup or hot chocolate could take more than an hour to prepare.

Perry had come to detest this whole ritual. Just

being in the thin air and low atmospheric pressure felt like a debilitating flu. *Who wants to eat and drink when you're sick as a dog?* he thought to himself. *Especially when you have to slave to boil water.*

The simple truth was that Perry was not the most gung-ho climber in the group. He had only qualified for the team because his uncle, Joe Sullivan, was the founder and president of Summit Athletic.

Even now, at twenty-six thousand feet, probably dying a little with each bottled breath, Perry was amazed that he had never said those simple words to Uncle Joe: *I don't want to go.*

It wasn't that his uncle was a tyrant. But the same force of personality that had built a multibillion-dollar empire had created a man who wouldn't dream of seeking anyone's opinion. He was accustomed to being in charge. He would never think of asking, "Perry, do you want to go to Everest?" What climber wouldn't?

Perry wouldn't. And didn't. And he was disgusted with himself that he wasn't safe at home right now, instead of trying to boil water in a place where water wouldn't boil.

Sleeping in an oxygen mask was an adventure. Usually it depended on how exhausted you were. Most climbers never slept at all at Camp

Four. But even for those who succeeded, it was more like a series of five-minute catnaps in the course of several hours of icy discomfort.

Tilt was the exception. Not only did he sleep in his breathing rig — he snored.

Sammi bounced a plastic cup off the sturdy shape inside the bedroll. At only fourteen years old, Tilt was the second youngest of the group, but he was built like an NFL linebacker.

"Come on, Crowley! Lose the buzz saw!"

"Don't wake him up," Perry pleaded.

The red-haired boy would have given much to avoid Tilt's in-your-face sarcasm, if only for a few extra minutes. Tilt would not have won any popularity contests with the climbers or the guides. Even the friendly Sherpas steered clear of him after they learned that he referred to them as "baboons," a takeoff on Babu's name.

Eventually, they all found sleep, even Perry. His uneasy dreams placed him on a toboggan on an endless hill. The other riders were cheering.

What are they, crazy? Don't they see there's no bottom?

And then something shoved him hard from behind.

Caught in hazy semiconsciousness, he was still plummeting down when the force struck again. This time he saw what it was. Buffeted by the howling gale outside, the wall of the tent was *moving!*

A new and even more terrifying sensation followed — the nylon floor, skidding beneath them. He could feel the rock and ice surface of the Col passing below.

That was enough for Perry. He started screaming.

"Shut up, wimp — " Tilt began.

Then the world turned upside down. Overpowered by the wind, the light aluminum tent frame folded like a beach chair. And they were rolling.

"Do something!" howled Sammi.

But nothing could be done. Perry was immobilized in his sleeping bag, his face pressed against the tent floor. The others somersaulted over him as the four rattled around inside the nylon tumbleweed.

Trussed up and helpless, Perry could only estimate how far the gale was blowing them. If they rolled over the side of the Col, his toboggan nightmare would become a horrifying reality. It would be a four-thousand-foot slide down the steep Lhotse Face.

"Oof!"

A heavy weight landed on top of them, and the tent stopped rolling. Scant seconds later, a knife blade cut through the windproof fabric, missing Perry's nose by an inch and a half. Cicero was there, hauling them out one at a time, while big Babu lay across the wreckage of the tent.

Perry stared, his thoughts a mixture of awe and relief. Another fifteen feet would have put them over the side of the Col and into oblivion.

The instant Babu released his grip, the wind launched the shredded tent high over the Lhotse Face. The SummitQuest team watched it soar like a kite until it was out of sight.

Hunched together for protection from the gale, they surveyed what used to be Camp Four. Not a single tent was still standing. Sneezy and Andrea Oberman, the expedition doctor, struggled to salvage equipment where the guides' shelter had once been. Not far away, the tents of This Way Up, another expedition, were in tatters.

Tilt was like a wild man. "Let's go *right now*! Once we bag the summit, the whole lousy mountain can cave in for all I care!"

"Tilt — *think*," Dr. Oberman ordered. "Even if we could climb in this wind, we've got nowhere to come back to. Camp Four is *gone*!"

"So we won't stop at the Col!" Tilt raved. "We'll go all the way down to Camp Three! We've got an early start! We can make it!"

THE SUMMIT

Cicero grabbed him by the front of his wind suit. "Get a hold of yourself, Crowley. You may be going to the summit someday, but not today."

Dominic spoke up. He was so small and so quiet that people often forgot he was there. Yet despite his youth and size, his climbing instincts were too good to ignore. "We should leave right away," he suggested. "As it is, we'll be descending the Lhotse Face in the dark."

The fear and shock in the group receded, leaving disappointed resignation. Their second failed summit bid. They knew the drill: a night at Camp Three, another at Camp Two on the Western Cwm, and then down to base through the treacherous Khumbu Icefall.

Sammi groaned into her mask. "I can't face Base Camp again."

"We're not going to Base Camp," Cicero informed her. "We'll head down into the valley."

Tilt's eyes bulged. "We're *leaving*?"

"We'll lose some altitude, breathe some decent air, get some real sleep." Cicero flipped up his goggles and regarded them intently. "Then we'll call up Summit and see if it's time for us to go home."

CHAPTER TWO

www.summathletic.com/everest/valley

Foiled by the mountain a second time, the youngest Everesters in history descend into the Khumbu Valley to the village of Gorak Shep, a day's trek from Base Camp. Here they await word from Summit Athletic headquarters. Is their adventure over?

The answer comes back a resounding "Climb on!" But Everest itself will have the final card to play. Is there one more window of good climbing weather left this season? The team can only wait and hope.

In the meantime, they force all tension aside and use this delay as a chance to catch up on the news back home. **CLICK HERE** to see the climbers chatting with families and friends on the satellite telephone — an example of how modern

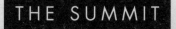

technology can transform a primitive setting.

"It's a pack of lies!" Cicero bellowed into the handset.

On the screen of his laptop computer was a newspaper article from the *National Daily*, E-mailed from Summit Athletic headquarters in Colorado.

MIDDLE SCHOOL HIJINX AT 27,000 FEET

The so-called mountaineers of SummitQuest continue to prove that filling a climbing team with children for the sake of grabbing headlines is more than just cynical; it is downright dangerous — not just to the teens themselves, but to other expeditions as well.

By far the most shocking example of this took place recently when thirteen-year-old, ninety-pound Dominic Alexis took injured climber Nestor Ali on a reckless 150-foot slide high on Lhotse, the fourth-highest mountain in the world. By the time the incident was over, dozens of climbers had risked their lives in rescue attempts, and Ali had to be airlifted to a hospital in a costly helicopter evacuation. . . .

"I saw that slide!" Cicero raged. "It was the only way to get the guy down from there. I don't know if I would have had the guts to do it myself!"

"Unbelievable," muttered Sammi to Dominic as Cicero raved into the phone. "I mean, you were the hero of that rescue. And they blame you for putting Nestor in the hospital."

"It's your fault, all right," added Perry. "Your fault he's still alive."

Dominic shrugged helplessly. "They're not lying, exactly. Everything in the article happened. It goes to show how the media can distort the truth just by the way they report the facts."

"I'll tell you what it shows, shrimp," sneered Tilt. "It shows that somebody hates us. And we all know who's got the most to lose if we summit."

Sammi made a face. "Ethan Zaph."

The famous Ethan Zaph was a member of the This Way Up team and the current record holder as the youngest alpinist ever to conquer Everest. If any of the SummitQuest climbers made it to the top, that record would be broken. Someone was feeding the *National Daily* embarrassing and misleading information about SummitQuest. Sammi was pretty sure she'd found the culprit.

Dominic did not agree. "How could it be Ethan? He was one of the guys we rescued."

"Yeah," agreed Tilt. "And isn't it convenient that rescuing those two kept us off the summit so his precious record could stand forever?"

Even Sammi didn't buy that theory. "I don't think he faked it; I just think he's a rat!"

Tilt made no reply. He was the only one of them who knew for certain where the *National Daily* was getting its information. At first, he had done it strictly for the money. Not everyone had a billionaire uncle like Perry. And climbing gear and clothing was expensive stuff — more than a lousy paper route would pay for.

But lately a second motive had taken over his secret E-mailed reports to the *National Daily*. Tilt's plan was to become the new Ethan Zaph — a younger summiteer who would win even more fame and fortune. There was only one problem: Dominic was even younger than Tilt. If he summited, too, *he'd* be the new record holder, and Tilt would be downgraded to also-ran. Who cared about the *second* youngest guy to bag Everest?

Dominic could make it, too. The shrimp led a charmed life, as if he'd been sprinkled with fairy dust or something! Every move he made turned out to be the right one; everybody loved him; the Sherpas treated him like a cherished younger brother. The only thing he *didn't* have going for him was the fact that he was young and small. And Tilt made sure that the *National Daily* hammered that piece of information into the public's head. Now a lot of people felt that Summit Athletic had put a baby on a mean mountain.

The fact that everyone blamed the *National Daily* on Ethan Zaph — well, that was just gravy. If Cicero ever found out Tilt was the leak, he'd be off the team faster than you could say Kathmandu.

Outside the window of this ramshackle excuse for a hotel, it was snowing. Every flake that fell here usually meant ten tons on the upper mountain. Tilt's brow clouded. None of this would matter if they couldn't get another chance to push for the summit.

Cicero slammed down the phone, fuming.

Sammi read his mind. "I say we head back to Base Camp and squeeze the truth out of Ethan Zaph."

"Forget it," said the team leader with a sigh. "In the next few days, we're either going up or going home. What possible difference could it make?"

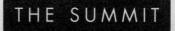

THE SUMMIT

CHAPTER THREE

Sneezy was E-mailing video footage from in and around Gorak Shep to Summit's Web designers in Colorado when he heard the helicopter. He was instantly alert. The villages of the Khumbu region were barely out of the Stone Age. High tech around here referred to the yak trains that ferried climbing equipment to and from Base Camp. A chopper meant business, and the only big business was Everest.

"Cap — "

Cicero was already at the window, watching the landing. "Here comes trouble," he said tersely.

The two men who strode across the hard dirt compound to the lodge wore paramilitary uniforms and black berets. They represented the government of Nepal, and had visited SummitQuest once before, at Base Camp. At that time, the articles in the *National Daily* had just come to the attention of the Nepalese climbing officials.

"Where's Dominic?" the cameraman whispered.

"Rock scrambling with Babu and Sammi in the hills," Cicero replied.

EVEREST

And then the men were ducking through the tiny door, their faces grim.

"Cap Cicero." The junior officer held out a murky faxed copy of the latest *National Daily* article. "The boy is here?"

"The boy is not here," said Cicero, tight-lipped.

"Where is he, please?"

"The boy is not here," Cicero repeated. "You've got something to say, say it to me."

"Three weeks ago, we came looking for the boy Dominic Alexis, and you told us he had departed. This was a lie, yes?"

Cicero shrugged. "The kid was sick. Then he got better."

"You assured us he would not climb," the man persisted. "And look what he did."

Sneezy spoke up. "He saved two lives."

"Which one cannot do unless one is on the mountain!" The young officer's irritation was growing.

"Enough of this hairsplitting!" snapped the ranking official. "Cap Cicero, we are here to inform you of a decision by our government. The boy, Dominic Alexis, is no longer on your climbing permit. He will not climb."

"You can't change the rules in the middle of the game!" exclaimed Cicero. "Nepal took big money from Summit Athletic for that permit. Dominic's on my team. If I climb, he climbs."

"Should that happen," replied the younger man, "you yourself, Cap Cicero, will be banned from climbing in Nepal. This would be a *lifetime* ban."

Cicero pointed out the window, where a long procession of heavily laden yaks could be seen coming down the trail from Base Camp. "In case you haven't noticed, the season is pretty much over."

"You cloud the subject well," said the senior officer. "But I hope you will listen well, too. This is not an idle threat, and we will not be fooled again."

The two uniformed men stalked back to their waiting helicopter, their military bearing slightly wilted by the altitude at seventeen thousand feet. Soon the chopper was airborne and gone.

Sneezy let out the long breath he'd been holding. "What are you going to do, Cap?"

The famous alpinist snorted. "You think I'm going to let a pair of tin-plated bureaucrats break up my team? What can they do — climb to the Col and arrest me? Did you see them? They were practically suffocating, and we aren't even at Base Camp."

"It's no joke," Sneezy insisted. "They're not

just two guys. They're a whole government. If you get banned, you're off Everest for good."

Cicero shrugged. "There are other mountains."

"But there's only one top of the world."

"You let me worry about that," said Cicero. "And don't say a word about this to anyone, especially Dominic. The kid's already stressed that the weather won't break. The last thing I want to do is mess with his head."

In the dingy dormitory room directly next door, Tilt Crowley took his ear away from the wall. He was smiling.

Dominic sprang fluidly up the lower slopes of the small peak Kala Pattar, planting his hands and feet with swiftness and authority. The freedom of this climb exhilarated him. Everest was the ultimate challenge, but there an alpinist was burdened by heavy equipment, footgear, and clothing. To do this — find some rocks and just go — was an undeniable pleasure.

He clamped both hands on a granite knob, chinned himself to the ledge above it —

And cried out in shock.

Strong hands grabbed him under the arms and hoisted him bodily up to the flat rock surface.

"Nice moves, shrimp."

THE SUMMIT

Dominic stared at Tilt. "What are you doing here? What happened to 'I only climb when it counts?' "

Tilt shrugged. "Gotta stay in shape." He took in his surroundings with an expression of distaste. "Pretty kindergarten stuff. You know — compared to where we've been."

Dominic nodded. "It's not exactly the Icefall. But think about it. We're over seventeen thousand feet. To get this at home, you've got to go to Alaska."

"Listen, shrimp, there's something you should know, because Cap's sure not going to tell you. Those two Nepal government guys were back this morning. You're off the climbing permit now. And they said if Cap takes you on the mountain, they're going to ban him from Nepal for life."

Dominic grew still. He had always considered that the *National Daily* articles could cause trouble for him. But never had it occurred to him that his problems might harm the career of a legend like Cicero.

Cap Cicero. That name had always been spoken with reverence around the Alexis home. Perhaps America's greatest living alpinist. Even now, after months together, it blew Dominic's mind that he was actually climbing with the man.

"You know," Tilt went on, "Everest is a big adventure for you and me. But for Cap, it's his living. If he gets kicked out of Nepal, it's not just good-bye, Everest. Three quarters of the world's highest mountains are right here. It would ruin him."

"It's not fair," Dominic said quietly. "If their problem is with me, why take it out on Cap?"

Tilt laughed mirthlessly. "Not fair! It's their country and their mountain, so they get to jerk everybody around all they please."

Dominic sat down on the hard granite of Kala Pattar. From here, Everest's triangular west side loomed over the valley, its cold indifference taunting him. The upper third of the mountain was shrouded in gray mist — a mammoth snowstorm, no doubt. The summit was still unreachable.

But even if that blizzard passed, opening up a window of clear weather, and even if SummitQuest took one final stab at the top, Dominic Alexis would not be with them.

The thought pained him grievously, bringing tears to his eyes. He could not remember ever wanting anything as much as he wanted to stand on that summit.

But it would never happen. He could not — *would not* — be the factor that ended the career of the great Cap Cicero.

CHAPTER FOUR

SummitQuest subscribed to five international weather forecasting services. They all called within the space of half an hour. The British were first with the good news: The impossible had happened. There was no monsoon, at least not yet. The jet stream was pulling north of the mountain, creating a pocket of clear weather that would be over Everest in two days. It would be brief, but a team with the right timing would have just enough of a window to push to the summit and get back down again.

"We've got our shot!" Cicero crowed ecstatically.

The news touched off a flurry of activity in Gorak Shep. They were still a day's walk from Base Camp. They had to leave immediately in order to be in position to take advantage of this gift from the climbing gods.

As they trekked up the path along the lower Khumbu glacier toward Base Camp, Perry's feet dragged on the moraine. Of all the lousy luck in the world, this had to win the Kewpie doll! He had rooted so long and so hard for the monsoon to come and end his hideous adventure. Even now, as they could physically see the blizzard moving off the peak of Everest, he still couldn't bring himself to accept the fact that they had a go. Again!

When they arrived at Base Camp late in the day, the place looked so different that it was almost a shock. So many tents were gone, so many camps deserted. Three weeks before, this settlement on the lateral moraine had been a bustling city of more than five hundred climbers and staff. Less than a quarter now remained — the diehards who had waited against all odds for this one last shot at the top.

So far, this had been the worst Everest season in recent memory. Not one single climber had reached the summit. If that pathetic statistic held, it would be the first time since 1977.

In the cavernous SummitQuest kitchen tent, Cicero briefed the Sherpa staff on what was to come. The climbing Sherpas were to leave before first light to repair the ladders and fixed ropes, and to rebuild Camp Four, which had been destroyed in the windstorm. The summit push would begin the morning after. There would be no margin for error. This late in the season, the good weather simply could not hold. Any delay would spell an end to their chances.

THE SUMMIT

A group of Sherpas from other expeditions came over to welcome Dominic back to Base Camp. Pasang, who worked for This Way Up, confirmed that his team would also be launching a last-ditch summit attack.

"Is Ethan going up?" asked Dominic.

Pasang nodded. "But this time climb with oxygen. Safer." Most Sherpas spoke with heavy accents. Babu was the exception.

"Gee, what was his first clue?" Sammi asked sarcastically. "When we had to drag him down Lhotse like a sack of potatoes?"

Pasang looked wounded. He had been climbing with Nestor and Ethan that day, and blamed himself for their mishap.

"She doesn't mean anything by it," Dominic told him apologetically. "She still thinks Ethan's behind all the trouble with that newspaper."

"And what about you, little sahib?" Pasang asked, using the nickname the Sherpas had bestowed on Dominic. "No monsoon, you get last chance. But no seem happy."

Dominic swallowed hard and said the words that he had not yet worked up the courage to speak aloud: "I'm not going."

Pasang's reaction was surprise; Sammi's was something more.

"What are you — crazy? This is what we prayed for! Of course you're going!"

"I'm not," said Dominic. "I decided yesterday."

"Why?" she demanded. "Because of the *National Daily*? Give me thirty seconds, and I'll go over there and feed Zaph his sat phone!"

"Keep your voice down," Dominic hissed. "Cap doesn't know yet."

"He does now!" exclaimed Sammi through clenched teeth. She marched off in search of the team leader.

Dominic watched her determined stride and knew she was going to rat him out. Sammi Moon never bluffed.

Pasang looked completely bewildered. "Why no climb?"

Dominic caught a quizzical look from Perry and an approving nod from Tilt. And then Cicero was bearing down on him.

The team leader didn't waste words. He grabbed Dominic by the wrist, hauled him out of the tent, and confronted him on the Base Camp rocks.

"This better be good!"

Dominic was close to tears. "I can't go. I'll cheer you guys on from Base Camp."

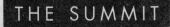

"Why?" Cicero bellowed. "Is it that stupid newspaper? Who cares what they print?"

"I had two shots at the summit and I can't face it again," Dominic lied. "I'm scared."

Cicero snorted in disgust. "I've seen you jump off a mountain in Alaska. I've seen you use a Himalayan peak like it was a kiddie slide. You're not scared of anything. Now I want the truth."

Dominic took a deep breath. "I can't let you get kicked out of Nepal."

Cicero was taken aback. "How do you know about that?"

"I hear things," said Dominic defiantly.

"Ask Babu about Nepalese climbing officials!" Cicero raged. "The Sherpas have a saying — I don't remember the exact words, but it translates to: 'Those guys couldn't find yak droppings in the middle of a herd of yaks!' "

Dominic was stubborn. "This could cost you your career."

"Good choice of words," the team leader agreed. "My career. Which means it's my problem, not yours. Listen, kid, I didn't want you on this team. I tried everything to cut you. But I couldn't because you're special. A lot of guys can tackle mountains and get to the top. But when you climb, the whole thing becomes larger than life, like it's a work of art! And every swing of your ice ax and kick of your crampons is a brush stroke. One of these days, they could talk about the great Everest heroes, Mallory, Hillary, Messner, and *Alexis*! It all starts right here, right now — if you'll let it."

But Dominic was adamant. He couldn't picture himself as a future climbing legend. The thought that Cicero, his own hero, saw him that way confused and flustered him.

But the fact remained: If he was responsible for the destruction of Cap Cicero, he would never forgive himself.

E-mail Message
TO: CalebS@zipnet.usa
Subject: All Systems Go!!

Dear Caleb,

Guess what? The jet stream moved off the summit. Or maybe the summit moved off the jet stream. I don't really understand which. Who cares? The point is WE'RE GETTING ANOTHER CHANCE!

It's four o'clock in the morning, but I'm way too amped to sleep. Caleb, it's so extreme up there that it makes

everything else we've done seem like patty-cakes. I wish you could go with me. We'd ROCK that hill — ha, ha. Get it? There's a lot of rock up there — you know, under all the ice. When I plant our picture on the top, I'm going to say, "You haven't seen the last of *this* couple!"

Keep your fingers crossed for me, Caleb. The second I hit the Icefall, I'm climbing in overdrive. The only way to beat an extreme mountain is to go totally ballistic.

Love,
Sammi

P.S.: I haven't heard from you in a while, so please E-mail back. How are exams coming along? I'll be in summer school to make up what I missed. Maybe you should flunk so we can go together (just kidding).

CHAPTER FIVE

The next morning, Dominic found Ethan Zaph in the This Way Up mess tent, sharpening his crampon points with a graphite file. The face that had adorned the cover of so many mountaineering magazines glanced up only briefly before returning to work. "Hey, Dominic. All set for tomorrow?"

Dominic swallowed hard. "I'm sitting this one out."

Ethan stopped filing. "Why?"

Even now, after two full days to get used to the idea, the words were difficult to say. "Nepal took me off Cap's permit."

"Because of the *National Daily*?"

Dominic nodded.

Ethan was distraught. "Dominic — I swear — it wasn't me!"

"I believe you," said Dominic. "Sammi and Tilt don't, but I do."

"You can still climb," Ethan told him. "By the time the Nepalese find out, you'll be off the mountain and gone. What can they do to you?"

Dominic shook his head sadly. "If I go, Cap gets banned from Nepal for life. And let's face it,

Nepal *is* his life." He reached under his collar and drew a thin leather strap over his head. On it dangled a small glass vial filled with sand. The necklace belonged to Christian Alexis, Dominic's older brother.

"It's Chris's," he explained. "Sand from the Dead Sea — the lowest point on Earth. He wanted to leave it on the summit. When he got cut from the team, he passed it on to me. And now that I'm not going — "

Ethan accepted the trinket, peering through the glass at the loose grains inside. " 'From the bottom of the world to the top,' " he said, quoting Chris's motto. He and Chris had climbed together. The American Junior Alpine Association ranked them numbers one and two, with Ethan in the lead after his conquest of Everest. He slipped the strap around his own neck and regarded the younger boy intently. "Why me? Why not give it to one of your teammates?"

Dominic shrugged. "You made the summit before. You've got the best chance of getting there again. I can live with not climbing" — a lie — "but I really don't want to let Chris down."

"I'll get it to where it needs to go," Ethan said confidently.

"Thanks." The look that passed between them plainly said that both recognized the truth — in the Death Zone, nothing could ever be certain.

The famous face wore a thoughtful expression as Dominic walked away.

E-mail Message
TO: Jsullivan001@summathletic.com
SUBJECT: Tomorrow's climb

Dear Uncle Joe,

You're probably going to kill me for this, but . . .

Perry leaned on the backspace bar, erasing the line.

I know it's crazy that I waited so long before telling you . . .

Another line disappeared from the screen of his laptop.

Are you sitting down? This may come as a shock . . .

Delete.

I DON'T WANT TO GO!!

He slammed the computer shut. *Tilt's right,* he thought sadly. *I am a wimp.*

Not because he was afraid of Everest. Any sane person would be. No, Perry was a coward for not having the guts to tell Uncle Joe the truth. Not even via E-mail from nine thousand miles away.

The SummitQuest camp was a beehive of activity as climbers and guides prepared for action. Wind suits were checked for wear, goggles and Gore-Tex mitts painstakingly counted. The word had just come over the radio from the advance team of Sherpas. They had arrived at Camp Two. The route was in good shape so far, although the days of heavy snow made for treacherous avalanche conditions.

The report had touched off wild celebration. Backslaps and high fives flew in all directions.

Perry stared at the scene of jubilation. *Wait a minute! Am I the only one who heard that?*

"Uh — excuse me," he said, tapping Cicero on the shoulder. "What was that last part? You know, about the avalanche conditions?"

"Oh, that." The team leader shrugged. "There's a lot of fresh snow up there. Sometimes it falls down."

That was what he had to say about the very real possibility of all of them being swept to their deaths by a tidal wave of roaring snow. Not that

Perry needed further proof that he didn't belong with these lunatics.

Of Perry's teammates, Dominic alone was untouched by the outbreak of summit fever. Perry didn't even try to conceal his envy. Once again, Dominic had a perfect excuse not to climb. And instead of being grateful, he was shattered.

Not shattered enough to change his mind, though. Perry watched as Cicero, Sneezy, Dr. Oberman, even Sammi begged him to reconsider his decision. Cicero was practically screaming: "Don't you dare do this for *me*! I don't care if I never see this stupid hill again as long as I live! I want you up there with me, kid!"

Dominic didn't budge. He had arrived at a course of action that he judged to be right, and he was about as movable as the mountain he now refused to climb. At five the next morning, when the rest of the team suited up and headed into the predawn chill, the boy didn't utter a word. He just waved, as if they were going next door, and not to the top of the world.

Cicero was flushed with emotion. "I'll get you back here some day, Dominic. As long as I've got something to say about what happens on this mountain, I'll find a way."

They started across the moraine. Dominic did not watch them go.

THE SUMMIT

A quarter mile along, they stopped to strap on crampons — boot attachments featuring twelve sharp metal points for biting into ice and hard-packed snow. They were surprised to see a helicopter parked on the thinning rocks near the entrance to the Khumbu Icefall. Two shadowy figures approached.

Sammi squinted into the gloom. "It's them," she confirmed. "It's those Nepal government creeps."

"He's in Base Camp," snapped Cicero as the younger official began peering into faces. "Are you happy?"

"Our concern is for young Dominic's safety first and foremost," the senior officer informed him.

"I'm all choked up," Cicero snorted, and led his team onto the ice.

The two government men waited until the SummitQuest climbers had disappeared into the blue crystalline wilderness above. Then, dizzy and gasping from the thin air, they piled back into the chopper and begged the pilot to get them out of there.

It was a thousand times harder than Dominic had thought it would be.

He lay in his sleeping bag, the heavy down

fabric tucked up to his chin despite the warming morning. Icy droplets rained down on him as the sun thawed out the frozen condensation in the tent. Khumbu water torture, the climbers called it.

No torture could compare with the agony of staying behind.

All at once the flap was flung aside, and light flooded the small shelter. "Suit up, Alexis," announced Ethan Zaph. "We've got a mountain to get on top of."

"No offense, but go away," Dominic grumbled. "You should be halfway to Camp One by now."

"I'm serious," Ethan persisted. "The Icefall gets unstable as the day heats up."

Dominic cast him a resentful look. "Don't pour salt in my wounds, okay? You know I can't climb."

"You can't climb with Cap," Ethan amended. "Nobody said anything about climbing with me."

"And I'm sure those Nepalese officials are going to see the difference," Dominic said sarcastically.

"Those Nepalese officials went home," Ethan pointed out. "But, yeah, they'll see the difference. How can they blame Cap when he doesn't even know you're up there? You'll climb with This Way Up, with our equipment, eating our food, sleeping in our camps. Nestor isn't here, remember? I can't think of anybody who deserves to take his place more than you."

Dominic stared at him, thunderstruck. It was true. Nestor Ali was home after a week in a Kathmandu hospital. There was a spot open on This Way Up. "But — " he managed, "you could get in big trouble."

"I *was* in big trouble," Ethan reminded him. "Three weeks ago, I was at 27,700 feet, flat out of steam, with an unconscious partner. And a thirteen-year-old kid convinced his team to come up and get us. Dominic, do you honestly think there's anything the Nepalese can do to make me worse off than I would have been if it wasn't for you? You saved my life; I'm saving your climb. Small payback, but you've got to let me."

Dominic rose on unsteady legs. He felt dazed, as if he had just woken up from a deep sleep. Convincing himself that his Everest dreams were over had taken so much willpower that he now considered it an unchangeable law of the universe: Two plus two equals four; Dominic doesn't climb.

Yet here was Ethan with an idea. . . .

"You were right," Ethan finished. "Nepal is Cap's whole life. But it isn't mine."

Dominic felt his brain and body coming alive

again as he examined the plan from every angle. It could work! If Cicero didn't even know he was on the mountain, how could the team leader possibly be held responsible? Dominic would just have to avoid the SummitQuest people at the camps along the route. They might bump into one another on the narrow ridges leading to the pinnacle. But that high up, they would be hidden behind wind suits, goggles, and oxygen masks — passing astronauts on a landscape so forbidding it would make the surface of the moon seem like a resort hotel. And anyway, in the throes of exhaustion, Cicero probably wouldn't even notice him. The team leader had said it himself: "Past twenty-eight thousand, you wouldn't recognize your own mother if she came at you with a Thermos of chicken soup."

Dominic regarded the bigger boy with tears in his eyes. "Give me ten minutes to get suited up."

"You've got five," said Ethan.

He was ready in three.

CHAPTER SIX

Mount Everest has claimed many lives in its history, but the Khumbu Icefall is its bloodiest battleground. Here the Khumbu glacier — really a frozen river — drops over a steep cliff. This sends millions of tons of slowly advancing ice careening down a half-mile escarpment. The glacier shatters into thousands of huge seracs, some of them the size of twenty-story buildings. It makes for spectacular scenery — a towering forest of jagged prisms the size of condominiums. But breathtaking as it is, the Icefall is not a place for sightseeing. The whole arrangement is moving, *falling*. The massive blue-white megaliths that lend the place its beauty might topple over without warning. Any unfortunate caught beneath an avalanching serac would be crushed like a bug.

A series of loud cracks punctuated the silence as hard glacial ice split and splintered beneath their feet. "Dangerous," Pasang said ominously. "No good climb so late in Icefall."

Ethan shot him a cockeyed grin. "You could have gone earlier. You wanted to wait for Dominic."

EVEREST

Pasang looked sheepish. There had been genuine dismay among the Sherpas when their "little sahib" had been grounded by the authorities. Pasang was privately determined to be at the boy's side all the way to the top. Dominic had many strikes against him, but the Sherpas of Everest were behind him one hundred percent. The SummitQuest Base Camp staff had even agreed to pretend he was with them whenever Cicero radioed in from the mountain.

"I'm just happy to be climbing," said Dominic. "All the way from Base, I was holding my breath. I half expected the entire Nepalese army to descend from the sky and arrest me."

"Well, they're sure not going to come looking for you up here," said Ethan. "So you're safe."

Crack!

A thin bridge of ice disintegrated beneath Dominic, and he was falling, dropping like a stone, straight into a crevasse. Desperately, he flailed with his ice ax, but he could not make firm contact with the dark wall.

He felt no fear, but only disbelief. Not that the mountain could kill, but that it could strike so fast — and without warning.

All at once, he came to a sudden jarring stop and dangled there, turning lazily.

The rope! he thought. *I'm still clipped onto*

the rope! Without it, he would surely be dead.

You're not safe yet! he reminded himself. *This line isn't made to handle that kind of jolt.*

"Dominic!"

He could barely hear Ethan's voice, although it was pretty clear that the older boy was screaming. "Dominic!"

He tried to yell, "I'm okay!" but it came out a high-pitched wheeze. He hacked madly at the glassy wall with his ice ax, but could not penetrate its smooth finish. He fared no better kicking with his crampons. Suspended in midair, he had no power behind his thrusts.

How can I get some of my weight off this rope?

His new teammates gave him the answer. Strong pulls on the line enabled him to get himself swinging. A stabbing kick with his right foot planted one front point; that purchase gave him the stability to stick the other.

With Ethan and Pasang steadying the rope from the surface, Dominic literally walked out. Pasang grabbed him by his wind suit and pulled him over the lip, where he collapsed on the ice.

Nobody spoke. There was nothing to say. There were certain near misses in mountaineering, mishaps that took climbers within a millimeter of disaster. Yet the only real damage they inflicted was to confidence. Physically, he was unharmed. This was exactly the same Dominic. Or was it?

"Okay," Ethan said huskily. "Your call. Was that a deal breaker?"

Dominic shook his head vehemently and panted. "Just give me a minute."

Ethan put an unsteady arm around his shoulders. Pasang squeezed Dominic's climbing mitt and would not let go. All three knew it had been that close.

www.summathletic.com/everest/abc

The final summit push begins with a day-long ascent, bypassing Camp One to Camp Two, or Advance Base Camp (ABC). Here in the radiant solar heat of the world's highest canyon, a team normally pauses for a day before taking on the upper mountain. But for the youngest expedition in Everest history, there will be no rest. Their weather window is razor thin, leaving no margin for error. They will climb tomorrow and the day after, followed by a summit marathon that will test them as they have never before been tested. **CLICK HERE** to see them preparing for one last shot at the peak. None of them will ever

THE SUMMIT

know such tunnel vision again. Every effort, every action, every breath is bent to the task of reaching the world's pinnacle. Not so much as a single thought is wasted on any other purpose.

Perry sat in the small tent, crouched over his laptop computer.

Dear Uncle Joe,

Before I set out for the highest point on the planet, there's something you should know: I'm no climber. What's more, I never was one.

It's not your fault, but in a way, it is. Because you never really asked how I felt when the crags got tougher and the cliffs got steeper. I just wanted to spend time with the uncle I idolized, and climbing was the way to do it. But somewhere in there, the cost of a mistake went from a few scrapes and bruises to my bones and maybe even my life.

Why couldn't we just stay home and play chess or something like that? Do

you even know I'm good at chess? I told you about fifty times. But you were determined for your nephew to have the alpine career you never got to have. This was always about you, not me. *Fortune* magazine voted you the sharpest CEO in American business. Yet you never even noticed that the higher we climbed, the less I looked down.

Well, Uncle Joe, where I'm going tomorrow, there's nowhere to look but down. There's a certain point where you get so scared that you just don't care anymore. I may not have the guts to stand up to you and save myself from the Death Zone. But I'm sure not going to march to that fate without making sure you know exactly how I feel about it.

He maneuvered the trackball over the SEND icon and hovered there, trying to work up the courage to put his message through. How many others had he written and deleted unsent?

All at once, the tent flap was flung aside and a laughing Tilt dove in, nearly flattening Perry. "I

just nailed one of the baboons with a snowball — direct hit, right between the eyes!" He spied the E-mail on the computer. "Hey, what are you writing?"

Red-faced, Perry slammed the screen shut. But the bully in Tilt was aroused. Whatever this was, Noonan didn't want it made public. And that meant that seeing it was a must. He made a grab for the laptop, but Perry pulled it away at the last second, taking the brunt of the big boy's lunge with his own body. The two went sprawling into the collapsible aluminum pole, and the tent came billowing down on them.

"*What's going on in there?*" Cicero's voice, not far away.

A second later, the orange nylon was snatched away, and the team leader stood over them, glaring down. "Anybody with sense," he seethed, "would have better things to do with his breath up here!"

"We were just fooling around," Tilt mumbled.

"Yeah, Crowley, you're a real fun guy," Cicero growled. "The next time I see you using the Sherpas for target practice, you'll be throwing your next snowball from Base Camp." From the remains of the shelter, he selected two large pots and shoved them into the hands of the combatants. "Go chop ice to melt for water. And not around camp, either. A hundred climbers have been using this place as an outhouse. I don't like surprises."

The team leader watched them storm off in opposite directions. Then he set about restoring the flattened tent. The first thing that caught his eye was the discarded laptop, which was jacked into the satellite phone.

The power light was on.

Perry got back first and placed the pot of ice chips on the camp stove. Then he turned anxiously to his computer. He frowned. It was off.

He booted the machine up again, but the message had disappeared.

I'll write it again, he thought urgently.

But he could already hear Tilt's crampons crunching on the glacier outside.

"Forget it," he mumbled aloud. His courage had vanished as completely as the E-mail he would never have been brave enough to send.

It was dusk when Dominic, Ethan, and Pasang marched into ABC. Dominic made sure to steer clear of the SummitQuest camp. He did catch a glimpse of Sneezy filming the sunset, but the sight

depressed him. For months he had been part of this family, and now he was expelled, banished practically. He felt lonely and disconnected.

Except for Ethan, the This Way Up climbers ignored him as if he had leprosy. He was an illegal member of this team, and nobody wanted to risk trouble with the Nepalese authorities. Dominic understood, but he didn't like being an outcast.

When he thanked Angus Harris, the This Way Up expedition leader, for giving him this last chance at the summit, the burly Scotsman replied, "Sure thing, Nestor. Good luck up there."

Dominic just stared at him, bewildered.

"You see, when I look at my climbing permit, the name says Nestor Ali," Angus explained. "So that has to be you, if you catch my meaning."

"Got it." Dominic turned to walk away.

"Hey." Angus put a beefy hand on his shoulder. "If you happen to see the lad Dominic Alexis, tell him we'll never forget what he did for our people on Lhotse. He shouldn't take it personally if we're not sticking our necks out to be his best friend. He's aces with us."

"I'll give him the message," said Dominic.

CHAPTER SEVEN

The stone was the size of a cantaloupe. It fell from near the summit of Lhotse, and by the time it appeared out of the low overcast, it was traveling at close to two hundred miles per hour.

Babu saw it first and sounded the warning. "Rockfall!"

The climbers flattened themselves to the slope of the Lhotse Face. The lethal projectile rocketed into their midst, whizzing by a bare six inches from Sammi's ear.

"Missed me!" she sang out defiantly.

The Face was the most grueling part of the climb — a mile-long skating rink tilted sixty degrees. Its icy steepness could be safely attempted only by jumar, a device that allowed a mountaineer to ascend a fixed line, but locked up automatically in case of a fall. Each agonizing step gained six or seven inches of altitude along a single rope.

When Camp Three appeared, it always seemed close enough to touch. Yet the slant of the Face had a foreshortening effect. For two solid hours the image of the tents teased them, elusive as a desert mirage. Sneezy got there first and pointed his camera unsteadily down the incline as the others struggled up to the tiny platform chopped into the ice.

Meetings at Camp Three were held lying down with the climbers' heads sticking out of the tents, facing one another.

Dr. Oberman shone a penlight into the teens' eyes and began to ask a series of simple questions: "What is your address?" "How many seconds are in three minutes?" "Spell 'spaghetti.'" "What is your mother's maiden name?"

"Tilt doesn't have a mother," put in Sammi. "He was hatched."

"I've got a mother," growled Tilt. "And she could beat you to a pulp even easier than I could."

"If they'd let her out of solitary," Sammi returned.

"What are you laughing at?" Tilt boomed at Perry, who was snickering into his bedroll.

"They're fine," Dr. Oberman assured the team leader with a tolerant smile. "They're the same pinheads they were before we dragged them down to Gorak Shep."

"All right, we're still acclimatized," decided Cicero. "But no one can acclimatize to the summit ridge, so I want everybody on bottled O's starting now. We hit the Death Zone tomorrow, and we only get a few hours' rest before we push for the top. It's our last chance; let's make it count."

Later, Sammi hunched in her oxygen rig, the Scuba-like echoes of her breath resounding in her ears. She was bent over her laptop, pounding out a last-minute E-mail to her parents while waiting for the satellite phone to connect her to the Internet. The device became temperamental at altitude. Camp Four was even worse. Last time, Sneezy had waited over an hour to send his footage to Summit's Web designers in Colorado.

As if on cue, the link was established. Sammi blinked. There was a message from Caleb waiting for her. She clicked on it.

Hi, Sammi,

Sorry I haven't gotten back to you sooner. Things have been crazy around here. Not Everest crazy, I guess. But a lot has happened since you left for Kathmandu.

Remember Myrna Applebaum? It's weird — you know how we always used to laugh at her? Well, I met her

skateboarding a couple of weeks ago, and it turns out she's pretty cool. Her cousin runs the pro shop at that half-pipe in Lawton, so she gets a lot of practice and she's *awesome*! She's never been climbing, but I told her where you were, and we checked you out on the SummitQuest Web site. . . .

Sammi's brow furrowed as she continued to scan the message. For two weeks she'd heard nothing from Caleb. Now he finally E-mailed her, and *this* was what he had to say?

I'm at twenty-four thousand feet on Mount Everest. Why would Caleb think I care about Myrna Applebaum?

When the truth hit, she reacted not with shock or even hurt. It was pure amazement. *He's dumping me!*

Then, even more astounded: *He's dumping me for Myrna Applebaum!*

She was oddly sympathetic at first. She'd been gone for nine weeks now. A month of boot camp before that.

Her second thought was more to the point: *That jerk!*

If it comes down to being Caleb's girlfriend

or being extreme, it's a pretty easy choice to make.

She reached into her knapsack and came out with an eight-by-ten glossy photograph protected by a Zip-loc plastic bag. It was Sammi and Caleb skydiving. Their chutes hadn't opened yet, so the two were captured in free fall, hands tightly clasped.

Sammi didn't even look at him. It was her own blissful smile that saddened her. Her anticipation not just of this jump, but of a whole future that would never come to be.

Hey, loser — think you're going to the summit of E? In a single motion, she ripped the picture in half, cleanly separating herself from her ex-boyfriend. Then she folded his image into a paper airplane, and sailed it down the steep pitch of the Lhotse Face.

Not in this life.

When Sammi Moon hit the summit, it would be as a free woman.

Unlike the other campsites, there was no set location for Camp Three. The expeditions bedded down wherever their Sherpas chose to hack out platforms in the Face.

This Way Up's tents were carved into the

slope about sixty feet below SummitQuest's. Dominic, Ethan, and Pasang arrived around four o'clock and immediately began chopping ice to melt for soup and hot chocolate.

Dominic never saw the object that struck him full in the face. It was a terrifying moment because he was working unroped, and even a small falling rock could have swept him off the Lhotse Face. But the impact was light — a sudden slap.

"Hey!"

Then he noticed it, sitting in a rut in the ice — a small paper airplane.

Ethan was disgusted. "Real smart. You could put a guy off the mountain with a stunt like that."

Dominic stared at the image on the folded paper. "If I didn't know better," he said with a frown, "I'd swear that's Sammi's boyfriend."

He reached over to pick it up. But a gust of wind dislodged the airplane from the Face and sent it spiraling down toward the Western Cwm.

CHAPTER EIGHT

www.summathletic.com/everest/
yellowband

Trouble at 25,000 feet: SummitQuest cameraman Lenny Tkakzuk loses his goggles while filming in the inhospitable Yellow Band, a thick layer of crumbly limestone in the mountain's midsection. Here, in a wind-chill approaching –100° F, a climber's eyeball can actually freeze solid without protection.

Help comes from an unlikely source. A Sherpa from an expedition called This Way Up offers his own eyegear for the remainder of today's ascent to Camp Four. "Sherpas born in wind and cold," the happy-go-lucky hero explains. "No need goggles." **CLICK HERE** to see Pasang, the savior of the Yellow Band. It's nice to have friends in high places!

Dominic lay on his stomach, shivering against the mustard-colored rock. Staying active was the climber's first line of defense against the blistering cold of this altitude. What was going on up there? He couldn't make out the problem that had stopped SummitQuest in its tracks.

Ethan returned to report that the coast was clear. "Pasang had to lend Sneezy his goggles. Let's give Cap a head start and then get moving again."

Dominic nodded, his teeth chattering into his oxygen mask. The brutal chill penetrated deep into his gut, and his fingers felt useless, like fragile porcelain attachments. Ten minutes later the team resumed its climb, and he warmed a little, but his core was still ice.

"You wanted to see me, Cap?"

Perry ducked out of the merciless cold into the guides' tent at Camp Four. He frowned when he saw his open laptop on the communications table. "What are you doing with my computer?"

"Sorry for minding your business, Noonan." The team leader waved the red-haired boy in front of the small machine.

Perry looked around in bewilderment. Dr. Oberman, Sneezy, and Babu were regarding him intently. "What's going on?"

"You'll want to see this, Perry," the doctor said gently.

Perry turned his attention to the glowing screen — an E-mail from Uncle Joe:

Perry, why didn't you tell me? You mean more to me than all the summits in the world! I had no idea you felt this way.

Turn around and get off that mountain. Call from Base Camp, and I'll send a chopper to pick you up. My plane will be waiting at the Kathmandu airport. I'll make this up to you if it takes fifty years. . . .

"I sent your message from Camp Two," Cicero explained softly. "Part of my job — never climb with a client who doesn't want to be there."

Perry sat stunned, reading and rereading the E-mail. It was hard to believe that this whole nightmare was over. Nine weeks of discomfort, deprivation, backbreaking effort, and insane risk-taking. Plus a month of boot camp. And now — a few paragraphs over the Internet, and he was done.

I'm going home.

The relief that washed over him wasn't as

sweet as he'd expected it to be. What a waste! The time. The effort. The *fear*.

"You can start down with one of the Sherpas in the morning," Cicero went on. "Let me say one thing first: I didn't pick you. But you've turned into a heck of a mountaineer these past two months. You're as tough as anybody here. Maybe even tougher, because you had to suck it up for every step. I'd climb with you any day."

The guides nodded their agreement.

Perry was silent for a long time. Then he said, "I guess I should go pack my stuff."

His computer under his arm, he crossed the seven feet of gale-force wind that separated the two tents. Ferocious conditions.

Not my problem anymore.

"What's up?" asked Sammi.

"I'm going home." The words sounded strange — somehow unreal. "They're sending a helicopter to Base Camp for me."

She nodded distractedly and said nothing. Perry recognized her game face under the oxygen mask. Sammi's focus was made of the same titanium as her ice ax.

Not so Tilt. As Perry gathered his personal items together, the big boy kept up a gloating, I-told-you-so monologue.

"Oh, poor Perry, he can't hack it on Mount

Everest. The other kids are mean to him — he has to go crying home to Mommy. Uncle Joey, send a helicopter, send your Learjet — "

Perry was smoldering as he jammed a sweater into the pack. The words formed in his mind: *Shut up! Shut up!* But he didn't have the guts to say them aloud.

"What took you so long?" sneered Tilt. "I could have told you on day one of training camp: This wimp couldn't climb an anthill, let alone the highest mountain in the world!"

Cheeks flaming hot as his bright red hair, Perry wheeled on the bigger boy. And this time, the words did come: "Shut up, Crowley!"

Tilt was taken aback at first. Then his features relaxed into an unpleasant smile. "Who's gonna make me, Noonan? You?"

Perry set his jaw. There was only one way to quiet Tilt. And only one way to undo the waste of these past months. To make this miserable experience mean something.

The E-mail would be short and to the point. And this one he *would* have the guts to send: **Dear Uncle Joe –** *not yet***!!**

Perry Noonan was going to climb.

THE SUMMIT

CHAPTER NINE

The plan was for a ten-thirty P.M. wake-up. Tilt was up by nine forty-five, melting ice for oatmeal.

He could not remember ever being this nervous. Tonight was the first night of his future. The blueprint for his life began right here, right now. Or not, if he messed up.

He wouldn't. He had been a monster on the climb up to the Col. Cicero had forced him to put on the brakes to keep from leaving the others far behind. He was in top shape, top acclimatization. He was even getting good at the eerie Darth-Vader breathing of bottled oxygen.

Besides — and this was the best omen of them all — the shrimp was down at Base Camp. Dominic's amazing luck had run out. Surely that meant Tilt was bound for greatness.

Sammi and Perry awoke, and Tilt made them breakfast. Why not? He had to do something to keep busy or the butterflies in his stomach would devour him from the inside.

Cicero came in for some last-minute nagging. "I want to see three layers on your hands — ny-

EVEREST

lon gloves, wool mitts, Gore-Tex mitts. You're not getting out that flap till you show me."

Normally, Cicero's control-freak personality drove Tilt crazy. But this time, he stood quietly and let the team leader check every piece of gear and clothing.

"Just keep doing what you've been doing, Crowley. You'll make it."

"Thanks, Cap." It was the friendliest exchange that had ever passed between the two of them.

Since Tilt was ready early, it was decided that he would set out ahead of the others. Sneezy would accompany him. That way, SummitQuest would take its best shot at the peak early, with its cameraman on hand to film the triumphant Tilt standing on top of the world. Then, on the way down, Sneezy could hand the camera to one of the other guides as the second team passed them en route to the summit.

As Tilt waited for Sneezy on the rocks of the Col, he was surprised to see another alpinist braving the battering wind. He knew that two other teams were launching bids tonight — This Way Up and the Germans. But both of those expeditions were known for late starts. Who was this?

The slight figure wore a Gore-Tex mask, full

oxygen rig, and goggles. It had to be a woman, and a little one at that. He was doing a mental inventory of female climbers when it hit him. The bright red wind suit. The small boots and crampons. The oversized ice ax.

Tilt moved closer, peering into the goggles. "Shrimp?"

The figure began backing away.

"Shrimp, it's me! Tilt!"

"*Shhh!*" Dominic pushed the oxygen mask aside so his warning could be heard. "Cap doesn't know I'm here!"

"*Why* are you here?" hissed Tilt. "How did you get here?"

"I'm climbing with Ethan Zaph," Dominic explained urgently. "Cap can't know so he won't be held responsible."

The frustration threatened to detonate Tilt like a grenade. Dominic Alexis! Somehow, the kid had managed to pull yet another rabbit out of his little runt hat! And here he was on the Col, poised to ruin Tilt's plans.

"Promise you won't tell," Dominic insisted. "Give me your word."

Telling Cicero — that was exactly what Tilt should do. But would it work? The team leader would never let Dominic quit so close to the top. Not even if he had to strap the shrimp onto his back and carry him kicking and screaming up the southeast ridge.

There was no way to keep Dominic from climbing at this point. What Tilt had to do was to find a way to prevent him from summiting. But how?

All at once, he had the answer. "The secret is safe with me," Tilt promised. "Listen, shrimp, I know we've had our problems. But I'm really glad you're getting your shot. Good luck tonight." He wrapped his arms around the smaller boy in a show of support.

"You, too," said Dominic.

As the young climbers embraced, Tilt reached around Dominic's back, found his oxygen regulator, and twisted the dial to maximum.

He broke away. "Hey, here comes Sneezy. You'd better not let him see you."

Tilt watched Dominic melt into the shadows. Gobbling bottled gas at a rate of four liters per minute, the shrimp would run out of oxygen by twenty-eight thousand feet, still more than a thousand below the summit. Cold, exhausted, and starved for air, he'd have no choice but to give up and return to Camp Four.

T

CHAPTER TEN

Dominic watched furtively as Sneezy and Tilt ascended the steep slope above the South Col. He squinted, trying to tell if they were front-pointing or climbing flat-footed. In the gloom, all he could make out were the hovering globes made by their helmet lamps glowing on black rock and white snow.

Where were Ethan and Pasang? It was dangerous to spend so much time standing around in brutal conditions, although Dominic felt surprisingly warm and strong. He had no way of knowing this was largely because he was breathing double the usual amount of supplemental oxygen.

Ethan wasn't at the tent, so Dominic headed for the This Way Up Sherpas' camp in search of Pasang. Inside, he found his Sherpa friend flat on his back with Ethan kneeling over him. When the beam of Dominic's helmet lamp penetrated the small shelter, Pasang cried out in agony.

"Douse that light!" ordered Ethan.

The tent went dark. "What's wrong?" Dominic asked anxiously.

The Sherpa's eyes were squeezed so tightly

shut that beads of sweat stood out on his fore-head.

"Snow blindness," Ethan explained gravely.

Dominic was shocked. "How?" But he already knew. Pasang had climbed without goggles from the Yellow Band to the South Col. His eyes had survived the cold; the bright sun was another matter. This high up in the atmosphere, there was virtually no protection from ultraviolet radiation. The glare of a cloudless morning, reflecting off ice and pristine snow, had blinded Pasang. Although the condition was only temporary, the Sherpa's ascent was over.

Ethan was furious. "You know better! Why'd you do it?"

The guide shrugged miserably. "Sherpas' life very hard. Many climb, but only few jobs. But if Pasang on Summit Web site, maybe sahibs want hire this Sherpa."

Dominic put a hand on his shoulder. "It's okay. We understand." He had become so close to the Sherpas that he saw them merely as new friends. It was so easy to forget their poverty. Pasang was not a fellow adventurer. He was eking out a living the only way he knew how.

"I let you down, little sahib," he moaned to Dominic. "And my team. And myself."

Ethan tried to put a good face on it. "You've

been up there three times already. You're hogging the summit! Give somebody else a chance, will you?"

"Go," urged Pasang. "Climb summit. I make tea when you return Camp Four."

"You sure you're okay?" asked Dominic.

"Go *now!*"

Dominic ducked out the flap and immediately ducked back in again. "It's Cap!" he hissed. "The whole team!"

Pasang had an idea. "There is" — he racked his brains for the words — "shortcut. Far west where Col curves down Lhotse Face. Much steep first, then simple walk to Balcony."

At 27,600 feet, the Balcony marked the start of the southeast ridge, the highway to the peak.

"If we can beat them to the ridge, we won't meet them again till we're on the way down," Dominic said excitedly.

The traverse to Pasang's shortcut was an easy ten-minute hike. There, at the northwest corner of the Col, Ethan and Dominic got their first glimpse of the Sherpa's definition of *much steep*. The "route" took them straight up a sheer cliff. It was so punctuated with both solid ice and naked rock that crampons would be a necessity one minute and a hazard the next.

"Pasang's going to owe us one first-class cup of tea," Ethan muttered.

There were no fixed lines. The two boys roped themselves together in the traditional style.

Their progress was exhausting and agonizingly slow. They inched up the wall, painstakingly placing CAM units and ice screws as they took turns belaying each other. An hour later, they had ascended a grand total of sixty feet.

Perry should be here, Dominic reflected, releasing a spring-loaded CAM in a small crack in Everest's hide. *This is his kind of climbing.* Dominic now respected the red-haired boy's rope work one hundred percent.

Ethan's fatigue and frustration were beginning to boil over. "Shortcut? *Nightmare* would be more like it! By the time we hit the ridge, everybody and his grandmother will be in front of us!"

Dominic could only shrug miserably as he struggled up the wall. A summit bid was a race against time. With every tick of the clock, the top of the world, in a sense, moved farther and farther away.

Only a quarter mile to the east, Sammi, Perry, Cicero, Dr. Oberman, and Babu were making much better time. They attacked the massive rock buttress of Everest's summit pyramid through a shallow gully. The terrain was not overly difficult, but the route was unroped, and the ice was like shatterproof glass. All was well as long as their crampons bit. If not — Perry didn't want to think about that.

Not thinking turned out to be a fairly easy thing to do. This high up, brain function was so impaired that thoughts were awkward and sluggish — if Perry managed to think at all beyond his movements. There was a brutal, yet strangely comforting simplicity to a summit push. This was no place for philosophers. The meaning of life lay in placing one foot in front of the other.

Fatigue came quickly. The South Col was barely out of the range of his helmet lamp, yet every few steps brought him to a standstill, leaning on his ax as he sucked breathlessly at his oxygen mask.

Cicero's reminders were gentle but firm. "You've got to climb faster, Perry. This expedition could put the youngest climber ever on that summit. But we could also summit the oldest if you don't hurry up."

Ten yards ahead, Sammi and Dr. Oberman were also flagging under the crushing effects of altitude. Her face contorted in a determined grimace, Sammi refused to rest, attacking the mountain with every cramponed step.

Only Babu seemed immune to the impossibly thin air of the upper mountain. Doubly amazing was the fact that he climbed without oxygen.

The guy's not human, Perry thought to himself. He kept an eye on the altimeter on his watch: 26,800 . . . 27,000 . . . 27,200 . . . Every vertical foot put more of a spring in Babu's step. They were almost at the Balcony. If this kept up, he'd be doing cartwheels on the summit!

Perry was never sure exactly how it happened. It wasn't a trip; not even a slip, really. But somehow, his crampons lost their purchase on the sheer ice.

When he first went down, he wasn't that scared yet. It felt like a routine skid, one of many on an icy climb. It was only when he became aware of the wind rushing past him, saw the blur of his surroundings flashing by in the gyrating glow of his helmet lamp, that panic set in.

He thought he heard Cicero's voice: *"Perry!"* But it might have been wishful thinking, his mind conjuring up the one person who could save him.

In a desperate attempt to slow his acceleration, Perry dug his crampons into the rime. His downward momentum stopped abruptly, and his slide became a head-over-heels tumble. Jolted and dizzy, never knowing which way was up, he closed his eyes and waited for his life to end. Would it be the rocks of the Col that snuffed him out? Or worse, would he be pitched down the seven-thousand-foot Kangshung Face? Or the four-thousand-foot Lhotse Face?

For God's sake, what difference does it make?

The jolts and bumps seemed to fade into a full-body numbness. All he knew was speed as gravity hurled him off this mountain he hated, and would now never escape.

Suddenly, he was airborne, flung by a ramp of ice. Those few seconds aloft brought with them a soul-crushing horror. For there was no way of telling if he was a few feet off the frozen slopes, or a mile and a half above the Kangshung glacier.

At the last second, he saw in the light of his helmet lamp the icy rock outcropping that swung up to meet him. The torch shattered. The universe went dark.

CHAPTER ELEVEN

www.summathletic.com/everest/
southeastridge

From the Balcony at 27,600 feet, the route to the summit follows the treacherous southeast ridge, a knife-edge of sloped rock more than five miles in the sky. It is one of the most lethal places on Earth. Huge snow cornices follow the line of the ridge, making each step a life-or-death gamble. Is there solid mountain underneath the drift, or are you stepping off into thin air? **CLICK HERE** to see fourteen-year-old Tilt Crowley breaking trail for his teammates to follow. A quarter mile above him, the summit waits. . . .

Sneezy slung the camera back over his shoulder and stumbled forward to catch up to Tilt. The guide had climbed Himalayan peaks before, but never had he experienced the hammer-blow effects of altitude like here on Everest. At twenty-

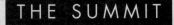
THE SUMMIT

eight thousand feet, they were higher than all but three of the world's mountains. Even with bottled oxygen, it was almost impossible to breathe. Panting, wheezing gasps were the best he could manage. His legs weighed forty tons each.

In spite of this, Tilt was moving onward and upward at an astounding pace. The teenager's strength was unbelievable. *He must smell it,* the guide thought to himself. *He knows he's going to the top.* Sneezy couldn't see anything standing in Tilt's way — certainly not Mount Everest.

"Hey!" he yelled. "*Hey!*"

Tilt held up, and a burst of tortured steps brought Sneezy alongside his charge.

"Slow down," he rasped. "If you summit without me, who's going to prove you got there?"

Behind the goggles, Tilt's eyes burned as if with fever. "Sorry. I'm just pumped! We're making great time, right? It isn't even sunrise yet."

Sneezy nodded. "If all goes well, it'll happen. What's going on in your mind, kid?"

Tilt grinned. "You have no idea."

The truth was that Tilt's thoughts were not with himself, but with Dominic. By the time the shrimp reached this altitude, he would be out of oxygen and forced to turn back.

The record would belong to Tilt.

*　　*　　*

Dominic lost track of time on the wall. It seemed endless, a vertical marathon that could only be tackled a single agonizing handhold at a time. Once he caught a glimpse of his watch and realized in dismay that four and a half hours had gone by.

Where's the ridge? he thought desperately. Could they be squandering their summit chances on this miserable cliff?

Fifteen feet above and to his left, he heard Ethan screaming with frustration — an almost unforgivable waste of energy and oxygen. Such was the anguished anxiety of feeling their bid slipping through their fingers.

The top of the wall never came. Instead, it rounded infuriatingly slowly into a mammoth buttress up against the upper mountain.

Weak and disoriented, Ethan and Dominic crawled atop the rock shoulder and took stock of their position. The ridge was nowhere to be found. Had they wasted this gargantuan effort?

Then Dominic saw it in the beam of his helmet lamp — a narrow arête carved into the mountain itself, a gently rising ramp perhaps eight inches wide.

Their eyes locked. It was a big risk. What would happen if they followed this path for hours only to have it disappear into the mountain? But the alternative was even less appetizing. The only other direction was down.

Ethan took the lead, walking the tightrope of the arête by gingerly placing one foot in front of the other. Half an hour later, they were unable to see anything that looked like the southeast ridge.

Up until that point, Dominic had thought only of how this detour might affect their chances of getting to the top. Now his mind began to fill with a deeper dread. Were they getting themselves lost high on mighty Everest?

All at once, their path cut sharply to the left, rounding a notch in the mountain's bulk. The arête widened into a ledge, and they stepped onto —

"The Balcony!" they chorused, weak with relief.

Above them stretched the ridge. Dominic squinted at the trail plowed through the shin-deep snow. Were these tracks left by Tilt and Sneezy? Probably. But what about Cicero and the rest of the team? Surely, they were ahead by now. And yet the new powder didn't seem to be trampled enough to indicate the passage of so many climbers.

Where was everybody? Had something gone wrong?

In the Death Zone, there was no time to keep

tabs on anyone else. Just staying alive was a full-time job up here.

They placed their spare oxygen bottles on the side of the path for pickup on the way down. Then they set out along the southeast ridge.

Had Dominic bothered to check the gauge on the cylinder that was hooked into his breathing system, he would have seen that his supply of gas was less than a quarter full.

Perry regained consciousness to find himself staring up into a ring of bright lights. Two thoughts occurred to him: 1) *I'm not dead* and 2) *I've stopped falling.*

He heard strange voices around him. They were speaking another language . . . German?

The German expedition!

"Where am I?"

Stupid question! If you're alive, what difference does it make?

The Germans seemed amazed to see his eyes open. "You *live*?" said a heavily accented voice. "After such a fall?"

Perry looked at his watch. The altimeter read 26,718. He had slid and rolled the height of a fifty-story building! Now he lay on a narrow ledge of dark ice. Four inches to his left, the lower ramparts of the summit pyramid fell away into the Kangshung Face. Those few inches represented the difference between being here alive versus being eight thousand feet straight down in Tibet.

Another helmet lamp joined the group around him.

"Perry!" The voice was hoarse and breathless.

He focused on the man beneath the light. Even through the mask and goggles, he could see that Cicero's face was gray.

The sight of someone who cared — really cared — disintegrated the last of his control. The emotion burst from him like the opening of floodgates. The tears poured out — for the years spent climbing when he'd hated and feared it; for the things he'd never had the courage to say to his uncle; for the months spent on Everest, and in boot camp before that, culminating in this latest mishap, which had almost cost him his life.

Cicero gathered him up in powerful arms and moved him back from the edge of the abyss. Still sobbing, Perry latched on to his team leader as if he would never let go.

"It's over, kid," Cicero soothed. "You're going home."

CHAPTER TWELVE

Breaking dawn flooded the summit pyramid with radiant sun. The effect was almost unreal. The top of the world was coming into day. Beneath them, the rest of the Himalayan range was still draped in the dark of night.

Tilt barely noticed the mountain's light show. He stood with Sneezy just below the South Summit, where the fixed ropes ended. Their attention was focused on Everest's lesser pinnacle, fifty feet above them.

"This is as high as anyone's gotten this year," Sneezy shouted over the howl of the wind. "We'll have to fix line the rest of the way."

Tilt shook his head vehemently. "It'll take too much time."

Sneezy was surprised. "We're on point," he argued. "What about the team coming up behind us?"

"We don't even know they'll get this far," Tilt shot back. "I'm not risking my chance to lay rope for people who aren't coming!"

The cameraman was disgusted. "Eighty years of tradition on this mountain, but that's not as important as you getting your name in the paper! We made it this far because other people fixed routes for us. Now it's our turn."

"What do I look like — a Sherpa?" Tilt sneered. And he set himself to the steep snow slope.

"Come back!" Sneezy's dilemma was clear. Yes, the boy was acting selfishly and with disregard for every unwritten rule of mountaineering. But it was Sneezy's responsibility as a guide to stay with the kid. He was only fourteen! "You can't go alone!"

"Watch me!" Tilt tossed over his shoulder.

"Let me belay you at least!" Sneezy hurried up to join him. "That powder looks unstable."

The two roped themselves together and began their attack on the rise. Tilt took the "sharp" end, leading the way up. He burrowed his crampons and ice ax deep into the snow to make solid contact with the husk of Everest. From Sneezy's viewpoint below him, it looked more like swimming than climbing. But their progress was steady despite the dizzying altitude.

Twenty minutes later, the two heaved themselves through a natural half arch of rock and came to stand on the South Summit. The altitude was 28,700 feet: 450 feet higher than K2, the second-tallest mountain on Earth.

They were the first climbers this season to gaze up Everest's summit ridge.

The ridge was notorious in climbing circles. It was razor sharp and totally unforgiving. Your first wrong step would be your last. It was also unimaginably exposed — a daredevil's tiptoe between the Kangshung Face to the right and the Southwest Face to the left. Across this blew triple-digit wind gusts. But this year there was yet an added wrinkle. Two weeks of blizzards had coated this airless catwalk with a thick blanket of unpredictable shifting snow.

The homestretch began — slow, careful steps along the heavily corniced ridge. They remained roped together, but on this terrain, a belay was virtually impossible. A fall by one meant they were both gone. They used their ice axes as walking sticks to support them against fatigue and the onslaught of the wind. They knew that only one major obstacle lay in their path — a deep notch in the summit ridge that created a forty-foot cliff in the sky. This was the infamous Hillary Step, named for Sir Edmund Hillary, Everest's first conqueror.

Gradually, the snow-covered Step came into view. Hundreds of alpinists had faced it before. But to Tilt it was a message directed at him and no other: *One last battle and the war is won.*

THE SUMMIT

The two climbers looked up. Dozens of ropes stretched up the rocky gash, some of them half buried in the snow.

Tilt looked questioningly at his guide, but Sneezy shook his head. They had to resist the temptation to use these old lines. Years earlier, a solo climber at the end of the season had become entangled in the spaghetti of ropes. The following spring, his body had been discovered dangling from the Hillary Step, frozen solid.

Their climb had gone extraordinarily smoothly so far. But here, only two hundred vertical feet below the summit, Everest chose not to yield so easily.

Tilt started out, still in the lead, but he was impatient, and exhausted himself quickly. Sneezy tried next, a more measured, experienced approach. But he, too, was spent and gasping in a matter of minutes.

Tilt sat on the soft snow, glaring up at the Step with genuine malice. His dream would not end here, foiled by a glorified divot in the summit ridge. *You can't beat me! I won't be stopped!* And he was back at the rise, climbing it, almost wrestling with it.

Far on the right side of the notch, he found, beneath the powder, snow packed hard enough to support the front points of his crampons. Soon the points hit bare rock. But Tilt would not be denied. Jamming his ice ax into a crack, he grabbed on and literally chinned himself to the next handhold.

Watching from below, Sneezy was bug-eyed. At this altitude, the tiniest movement was considered a triumph. Tilt's display of arm strength was nothing short of miraculous. Fighting his own exhaustion, he brought out the camera. The world had to see this — the most storied obstacle in high-altitude mountaineering being conquered by raw power and sheer cussedness.

Roaring his defiance, Tilt scrambled atop the Step. Sneezy almost expected him to beat his chest and emit a Tarzan yell. But instead, he twisted an ice screw into the thick rime at the lip of the notch and dropped a length of nine-millimeter nylon line to Sneezy at the bottom. The guide tethered it to a second screw at the bottom. The Hillary Step was roped.

Slowly, but with growing excitement, Sneezy jumared up the rope. For him, too, this was a first ascent of Everest. The thrill was greater here than on any other mountain.

From here, the summit ridge looked like a gargantuan arrowhead of brilliant white rising above them. All detail disappeared in the gleam of the snow. Where was the top? Tilt couldn't see,

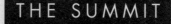

THE SUMMIT

but the route was obvious: Follow the ridge higher and higher — until there was no such thing as higher anymore.

The sky was mostly clear, but Tilt could feel tiny bee stings of ice on his face, the crystallized moisture that made up Everest's summit plume. The world was a different place up here near the edge of Earth's troposphere. Energy and exhaustion seemed to melt into each other. Here, there was only purpose. Tilt kept moving, one foot in front of the other, as if the summit were a magnet, pulling him ever upward.

Sneezy cleared the frost off the dial of his climber's watch. "Twenty-nine thousand feet!" he practically screamed. The number looked impossible, illogical, unreal.

They were almost there! They had to be! Tilt squinted into the glare. *Where's the peak? It should be right here! Is something wrong? Are we lost?*

And then the next step . . . was *down!*

CHAPTER THIRTEEN

It didn't register at first. *What's happening? The ridge goes up, not down!*

At that moment, Sneezy threw his arms around the youngest climber ever to summit the world's tallest mountain.

Tilt grabbed the guide's wrist and checked the number on the altimeter: 29,028. It didn't get any higher than that. Not on this planet.

The surge of joy that rose up in him reminded him of the depiction of a supernova that he'd once seen in a planetarium show — an explosion of white light growing in intensity as it radiated outward in waves.

He had done it! At this altitude, he had trouble wrapping his oxygen-deprived mind around the fact that he wasn't the same person who had awoken at the Col eleven hours ago. He was now living the very first minute of the rest of his life — he scanned the panorama — with the whole world literally at his feet.

The old Tilt Crowley, that ninth-grade nobody from Cincinnati, the one who earned money by delivering papers — he didn't exist anymore. Tilt was famous, a celebrity, a star. He was going to be rich.

Sneezy was shouting into the walkie-talkie. "We're here, Cap! We're on the summit! Right now!"

"How's Tilt?" came Cicero's voice.

"Strong — really strong! He led the Step like a pro! Where are you guys?"

"I'm at Camp Four," Cicero reported. "Perry took a dive."

"Is he okay?"

"Couple of broken ribs, Andrea says. Nothing serious. Sammi and Babu are on the southeast ridge. Let me talk to the kid."

The fourteen-year-old was still wild with excitement. "Cap, it's *amazing*! You've got to see it!"

"I've been," came the amused reply. "Now listen up. Andrea's already on the sat phone to Colorado. You're going to be in all the papers tonight. You ate this mountain for breakfast."

"Thanks, Cap."

"I know you feel like you're done for the day," the team leader went on, "but here's some advice you'd better take: A lot of climbers can get up that rock; the trick is to get yourself down again. So take your pictures, enjoy the view. Then get your butt back on the ridge, because you're only halfway there."

"Gotcha," replied Tilt. Nothing, not even Cicero's nagging, was going to spoil this moment for him.

He watched as Sneezy attempted to unfurl a Summit Athletic Corporation flag in the battering gale. From his apparently bottomless knapsack, the guide produced a telescoping aluminum flagpole. The two of them planted it in the snowpack next to the half-buried survey rod that marked the peak.

SummitQuest — Tilt had almost forgotten that he was part of an expedition. One that was an official success now that it had placed a member on the summit. A lot of credit would be claimed over this — by Perry's uncle, whose brainchild it was; Tony Devlin, who handled the business end; Cap Cicero, who led the team.

Take your bows, guys. I'm at the top, and I don't see any of you here.

This victory belonged to Tilt Crowley.

Babu put the walkie-talkie back in his wind-suit pocket and turned to Sammi, behind him on the ridge. "That was Cap. Lenny and Tilt are on the summit."

Sammi was astonished. "Already?" The two had been delayed by Perry's accident. They were barely beyond the Balcony. "Go, guys! They flew!"

THE SUMMIT

"They made good time," Babu agreed. "But mostly, we're way behind schedule."

"Then what are we waiting for?" She increased her pace and pushed past him, gasping into her mask.

"Sammi!" He had to scramble to keep up with her. "You know, Cap put a two o'clock turnaround on us." The turnaround meant simply this: If you weren't on the top by two P.M., it was too late to keep climbing. At that time, all team members had to head back down to Camp Four, regardless of their position on the mountain. If they did not, they would end up descending in the dark at a time when their headlamp batteries would be most likely to fail.

"It's not two o'clock yet," said Sammi, tight-lipped.

"If you climb too fast, you'll burn yourself out," he warned.

She tried to grin, but through the pain of her effort, it came out a grimace. "Come on, Babu. You know me. I've only got one speed."

And Babu did know her. Over the past two months, he had come to admire the girl's tenacity and fearlessness. But he also knew Everest. Perry's accident had cost them a lot of time. To make up that time, they would need determination, skill, and luck.

Babu Pemba had been in this game long enough to realize that very few climbers could count on having all three at the same time.

Ethan and Dominic were approaching twenty-eight thousand feet when they first saw the two specks descending the southeast ridge above them.

Ethan looked at his watch. It was only ten-thirty A.M. If those dots in the snow were coming from the peak, then they were climbing at near-record pace.

He frowned. "Did the Germans send an early summit party?"

Dominic shook his head. "That has to be Tilt and Sneezy. I'll bet they made it."

"Probably," Ethan agreed. "Tilt never did take no for an answer." He grinned. "I guess that means I'm not important anymore."

As the ascending and descending pairs closed the gap, Dominic could see that the lead climber above — probably Tilt — was moving strongly. His partner was having a much tougher time. Every two or three steps, Sneezy would slump on his ice ax to snatch a few seconds of rest. He wasn't in danger, exactly. But he wasn't doing well.

Half an hour later, the two teams passed.

Dominic pretended to lean forward into his climb, keeping his face averted. He didn't want Sneezy to recognize him and alert Cicero. He needn't have worried. The cameraman was so exhausted that he never moved his gaze from the narrow path in front of him.

Tilt, too, seemed content to let Dominic keep his secret. He confirmed their summit success with a single thumbs-up, and exchanged a high five with Ethan — the new record holder accepting the torch from the old.

Ethan put an arm around Sneezy and hugged the older man briefly. "One foot in front of the other, Lenny. That's all you have to do."

The guide could only grunt his acknowledgment and plod on.

Powering past, Tilt felt a pang of guilt. Zaph and the shrimp seemed genuinely happy for him. He almost turned around to warn Dominic that he was about to run out of oxygen, but fought the impulse down. Tilt was only in this generous mood because he now held the record. If the shrimp somehow managed to get his hands on a spare bottle of gas, and made it to the top, Tilt's time in the spotlight was going to be very short.

He reached out an arm to steady Sneezy, who was wobbling.

"Thanks," the cameraman panted. "Hey, was that Zaph?"

"That was him," Tilt confirmed. "The *second* youngest kid ever to summit Everest."

"Climbing with Pasang, right?" Sneezy persisted, trying to create order out of his jumbled thoughts.

"Yeah, Pasang. Right."

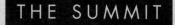

CHAPTER FOURTEEN

The ridge grew steeper as the sun rose in the sky. Ethan and Dominic slogged on, feeling the weariness as never before. Most Everesters agreed that this was the make-or-break section of the summit assault, the crucial second act of a three-part drama. The euphoria of reaching the Balcony has worn off, yet the next milestone, the South Summit, is a dangerous, oxygen-starved marathon away — more than one thousand vertical feet of unbreathable air, unbearable cold, and overpowering wind.

It was easy to despair at 28,300 feet. Here, higher up than all of the world's lesser peaks, the summit still seemed distant.

Don't think, Dominic commanded himself. He immersed his mind in the lore of history's great alpinists. All had doubted themselves on this jagged, inclined proving ground. Yet all had prevailed by following a credo that was so simplistic that it bordered on the childish: *Just keep moving.*

Suddenly, he was on his knees in the snow, struggling for his next breath. Desperately, he yanked off his mask and searched the plastic breathing tube for any sign of blockage. It was clear.

Ethan was at his side instantly. The older boy's eyes went straight to the tiny gauge on the oxygen cylinder. "You're out of O's!"

"That's impossible!" Dominic gasped. "I took a full bottle at the Col!"

"This thing's open to maximum!" Ethan exclaimed. "Of course it didn't last!"

"But — " The reply was fully formed in Dominic's head. He had personally set his oxygen to two liters per minute. Yet his brain could not communicate the words to his mouth. Confusion — that was another sign of hypoxia — oxygen starvation. The symptom that came next was even more alarming — a deep, whole-body chill that began in his fingers and toes and spread inward.

Ethan detached his own cylinder of gas and hooked it into Dominic's regulator.

Dominic took two deep breaths and then pushed the mask away. "You need this! I won't take it from you!"

Ethan shook his head. "I summited Lhotse without gas."

"We're *higher* than Lhotse!" Dominic argued. "And we're not done yet! We've got to descend to the Balcony and get our spare bottles!"

THE SUMMIT

"No!" Ethan wheezed. He hyperventilated for a moment as he adjusted to the thinner air. "If we go down, our summit bid is finished!"

Despairingly, Dominic knew it to be the truth. They were more than seven hundred feet above the Balcony. If they descended, every inch of that ground would have to be climbed again en route to the pinnacle. They would not have the strength. But mostly, they would not have the time.

"Let *me* go down," Dominic insisted. "This is my problem, and it shouldn't cost you your chance."

"This *is* my chance," Ethan countered. "The minute I hit the top last year, I knew one day I had to try this mountain without O's. I chickened out after what happened on Lhotse, but this is my wake-up call. If I don't give it my best shot, I'll be asking 'what if' for the rest of my life." And he hunched into the wind and continued up the corniced ridge.

Dominic watched for an uncertain moment and fell into line behind him.

He may not be the record holder anymore, Dominic thought to himself, *but he's already one of the all-time greats. I'm proud that he wants to climb with me.*

The wind shifted. Now it seemed to be blowing straight down from the top of the ridge, directly in their faces. Dominic found himself drifting ahead of Ethan. It was not so noticeable at first, but as they fought onward and upward, it became obvious that Ethan was losing ground. Without oxygen, the older boy was experiencing cold and fatigue much more acutely than Dominic. And every step drew them into even lower temperatures and even thinner air.

Dominic tried to slow his own pace to match Ethan's. It was easier said than done. In these conditions, movement and exertion were warmth and life; slowing down seemed as unnatural as the stately choreographed march of a wedding procession. Their progress dwindled to a snail's pace. It took them over two hours to get to the bottom of the steep slope of unstable snow that led up to the South Summit.

"Where are the ropes?" asked Dominic.

Ethan barely had the strength to shrug. "I'll lead."

It was like watching slow motion — Ethan, half buried in powder, wriggling up the fifty-foot pitch. He was about halfway to the top when it appeared to Dominic as if he had come to an abrupt halt. A moment later he was sliding down, his mitts still reaching for handholds. Had it not been for the sheer danger of their surroundings, it would have been comical — a scene from a Road Runner cartoon.

Dominic made the decision quickly. He shrugged out of his oxygen system and placed the mask over Ethan's mouth and nose.

Ethan recovered quickly. "Give me a minute!" he croaked.

Dominic shook his head. He fought off the feeling of strangulation and struggled to settle his own breathing. *You can do this,* he told himself. *You're acclimatized.*

He set himself to the slope. The first burst of effort brought on a head rush that very nearly flattened him. But it passed. He began to inch his way up, and as he ascended without oxygen, he gained confidence that it really was possible.

Breathe. Breathe.

Partway up, he paused and lowered a rope to Ethan, who secured it at the bottom with an ice screw. The coil of line seemed abnormally heavy, and threw off his balance. But he caught himself and did not slip.

Breathe. Breathe.

The half tunnel that led to the South Summit seemed close now. He moved toward it, climbing, wading, crawling. The nylon line paid out as he ascended, roping the slope. But he didn't allow himself to think about that. The key to climbing without gas, he was finding, was pure focus. The South Summit above wasn't just the most important thing in the world; it *was* the world.

And soon he was on it, dizzy and gasping, but there. He fixed the rope to another screw. Fifty feet below, Ethan clipped on his jumar and moved up to join him.

It was one-forty P.M.

Poised on the wooden rail of the Terrace Bridge, Sammi Moon peered down between the toes of her sneakers at the rushing river of the gorge below. She didn't hesitate. She was off the bridge headfirst, dropping like a stone. The acceleration was even better than she'd expected, and she hurtled toward the water with spectacular speed.

When she felt the bungee cord begin to stretch, she knew a moment of disappointment. No! Faster! Don't let it stop!

The water was only a few feet away. But the full elastic resistance was pulling her back now, and would soon yank her up again. She longed to dunk her head in that ice-cold river, but the line wasn't long enough. Just a few inches short . . .

"Sammi!"

THE SUMMIT

She turned around to complain to the manager about not getting her head wet, and found herself staring into the concerned features of Babu Pemba. An arctic blast reminded her of where she was — hanging by the teeth of her jumar off a rope fixed to a notch in the southeast ridge above twenty-eight thousand feet. Mount Everest, Nepal, Asia.

"It's two o'clock," said Babu gently. "We go down."

"No!" She hauled herself up the line, sliding the jumar along. It was an explosion of energy, a Herculean effort, the best she could muster. It gained her a grand total of eight inches against the mountain. The summit was still a thousand vertical feet away.

"We're at least five hours from the top," Babu explained patiently. "That's if the weather holds out." He gazed to the south. To the left of the pinnacle of Lhotse, now actually below them, the peak Ama Dablam was wreathed in overcast that hadn't been there that morning. "I don't like the look of those clouds."

"Five hours is nothing up here!" Sammi complained. "You can spend five hours melting a liter of water! We can make it!"

"We can make it *up*," Babu agreed. "Not down. Not in the dark. We turn around."

Sammi was outraged. "You don't come nine thousand miles and climb twenty-eight thousand feet just to turn around!"

"That's *exactly* what you do," Babu countered. "I've been on seventeen expeditions; I've summited nine times. What do you think happened on the others? I turned back."

"Tilt made it," she offered defiantly.

"Tilt was lucky. Nothing happened to slow him down. What about Cap? His attempt ended before the Balcony. Does that make him a lousy climber? Sammi, you're good enough to bag this mountain. But things happen."

"Not to *me!*" she exclaimed bitterly. "When I do stuff, I do it till it's done! I live life to the extreme!"

"Not here, you don't," Babu said firmly. "There's only one kind of extreme on Everest — extremely dead. I don't know — maybe it's possible to stand on that summit at nightfall and climb all the way down in the dark. I'm never going to find out, because I'd have to bet my life on it. And I don't bet that high. What we need to settle now is — do you?"

Tears stung Sammi's eyes behind her goggles. It was not her failed bid that upset her. It had taken this man from an alien world to teach her something that she should have known all along

— that these pursuits she considered extreme were not really extreme after all. Skydiving, snowboarding, bungee jumping — they were games, hobbies. But when presented with something truly life-and-death, Sammi Moon said no thanks.

She didn't doubt that this was the correct choice. But right now, the idea made her very sad.

She looked off to the south. "Yeah, you're probably right about those clouds."

And they started down.

Sammi carried her disappointment like an extra burden as they slogged along the ridge. Not summiting certainly didn't make the descent any easier, only shorter. It still called for exhausting effort. Supposedly, the air was thickening with every step. *Ha!* she thought. *That's a laugh.*

Babu was in the lead. He clipped onto a fixed rope and rappelled down a twenty-foot drop, expertly steering clear of the soft cornice below.

Sammi swung a leg over the lip and paused. To the left of the route, a pristine, forty-five-degree snowfield stretched downhill for almost two hundred feet. There, the ridge curled around, cutting it off and containing it. There must have been dozens of similar places in the Himalayas. But this one had come at exactly the right time.

She descended about halfway down the

drop. Then, "Hey, Babu!" She cut the rope with her ice ax, pushed off from the step, and swung out over the expanse of white. Letting go of the rope, she dropped to the snowfield, landing on the seat of her wind suit. The slide began on impact. She sailed down the slope in a blizzard of powder, shrieking in sheer delight all the way. As she had known it would, the ridge stopped her glissade, wiping her out at the bottom.

Awestruck, Babu watched her emerge from the billowing cloud, scramble up through the cornice, and rejoin the ridge far below. As his heart slowly began to beat again, he realized that the mountain the Sherpas called Jongmalungma had not defeated Sammi Moon.

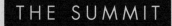

THE SUMMIT

CHAPTER FIFTEEN

Cap Cicero climbed from Camp Four and met up with Tilt and Sneezy a short way above the Col.

The cameraman was uninjured, but so physically weary that an extra arm to lean on was welcome indeed. "I'm fine," he kept repeating, over and over. "Just a little out of steam."

"And look at you." The team leader turned his attention to Tilt. He had never been a Tilt Crowley fan, and still wasn't. But he had to be impressed by the boy's achievement today. "You look like you're ready to tackle K2."

"I'm dead," Tilt admitted happily. "I'm just so psyched — I don't think I can sleep!"

"You'll sleep," Cicero assured him. "But I want two liters of liquid in both of you first."

The descent to the Col was steep and nerve-racking. Tilt found himself taking timid steps, as if he were made of delicate crystal.

What am I? he thought in disgust. *A wimp like Perry Noonan?*

The truth was that Tilt was uneasy because he now had so much to lose. His future was in the bag. He couldn't afford to be reckless.

At Camp Four, he and Sneezy downed steaming mugs of Sherpa tea while Cicero E-mailed the video footage of their summit bid to Colorado.

Then the new Tilt Crowley jammed himself into a warm sleeping bag and plunged into a dreamworld where every climbing magazine had his face on its cover.

He awoke three hours later, still exhausted, but too excited to stay in his bedroll. He had waited fourteen long years to be somebody. He wasn't going to miss a minute of this.

As he ducked from his tent to the guides', the blast of wind seemed almost bearable to him, compared with the howling gale of the summit ridge.

Inside, he found Perry and Sneezy, both fast asleep. Otherwise, the shelter was deserted. He picked up the sat phone from Cicero's gear and hustled it back to his own tent. There was a very important message to be sent.

Part of his secret agreement with the *National Daily* stated that, if he made it to the top, all fees would be doubled. It was time for the youngest summiteer in Everest history to start seeing some cash.

He booted up his computer and began to type.

THE SUMMIT

E-mail Message
TO: bv@national-daily.com
Subject: Did it!

Hit the summit today with guide Lenny Tkakzuk at 9:07 A.M. Perry fell and slid halfway to the Col on his butt. He's fine if you don't count broken ribs and gutlessness. Sammi and Dominic both quit before the top. Yeah, Dominic climbed after all with another team, but equipment problems stopped him around 28,000. . . .

The tent flap opened briefly, and Sammi dragged herself in, utterly spent from her climb. "Hey, Tilt, way to go!"

Startled, he slammed the computer closed to hide the incriminating E-mail. "Get out of here!"

She snorted. "I'm happy to see stardom hasn't done anything to change your sunny personality."

Tilt was chagrined. "Sorry," he mumbled. "You just kind of snuck up on me. How far did you get?"

"Not far enough," she groaned. "You know, you and Sneezy will probably end up the only ones to summit this season. Everybody else is turning around, too. The Germans never really got their act together. And the This Way Up teams are all heading down."

"How about that," chuckled Tilt. "The great Zaph turns out to be human after all."

Sammi frowned. "I didn't see Ethan. Are you sure he's climbing today?"

"He was going up the ridge when I was coming down! Him and — this other guy! But they had oxygen trouble. They should be at the Col by now."

She shrugged. "All I said was I didn't see him. He could be here." She yawned hugely. "I just wanted to say congrats. I've got to go get yelled at some more. I had a little fun on the descent, and Babu got all bent out of shape about it." And she wandered out.

It was a good thing that Sammi had been too bone weary to notice that Tilt had gone white to the ears. Ethan and Dominic *not back yet*? How could that be? The shrimp would have run out of oxygen eight hours ago! They could have *crawled* back by now!

A numbing dread growing in the pit of his stomach, he burst out of the flap and rushed over to the This Way Up camp, trying his best not to run. He found the returning climbers limp and disheveled, chugalugging vast amounts of tea and

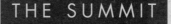

soup in an effort to hydrate themselves so they could lie down and pass out.

A few recognized him and called out their congratulations.

Tilt tried to sound casual. "When did Ethan get back?"

He got blank looks. No one could recall having seen This Way Up's most celebrated climber, either at camp or on the mountain.

Heart pounding, Tilt went from tent to tent. No Ethan, no Dominic.

"Ethan sleep red tent there," one of the Sherpas told him.

"Thanks." The two-person shelter was empty and had obviously been so all day. The stove was cold, and a tin cup sat on the nylon floor. It was half full of soup, now frozen solid.

Possibilities popped into his head, all of them worst-case. When the shrimp ran out of O's, he collapsed, and Zaph wouldn't leave him. Or he got lost, and Ethan was looking for him. Or he was so impaired that Ethan had to drag him, inch by inch, all the way back to Camp Four.

It didn't matter which scenario was the right one. None of this would be happening if Tilt hadn't tampered with Dominic's oxygen cylinder.

I only meant to turn the kid around, not kill him!

And now Ethan was missing, too, thanks to Tilt.

The irony of it nearly tore him in two. Here he was, at the greatest moment of his life, poised to drink in the sweet nectar of fame and fortune he had always craved. But how could he face himself, knowing that his success had been paid for with the lives of two innocent people?

If they die, I killed them!

A rush of adrenaline sent him pounding across the black rocks to his tent. He shook the layer of frozen perspiration out of his wind suit and dressed at lightning speed. Outside, he strapped on crampons and stuffed his pack with a walkie-talkie, spare helmet-lamp batteries, and two oxygen cylinders.

It occurred to him only briefly that it might be foolhardy to be climbing again so soon after a fourteen-hour round-trip sprint to the summit. The caution seemed far less important than the two alpinists he had deliberately put in danger.

Hang in there, shrimp! I'm coming to get you!

No one saw him hit the snowy slope. He was moving so fast that he was soon out of sight among the lengthening shadows.

CHAPTER SIXTEEN

The call came over the radio at six o'clock. Dorje, SummitQuest's Base Camp Sirdar and cook, sounded worried. A howling blizzard was dumping heavy snow on the Khumbu glacier. How were conditions at Camp Four?

Cicero peered through the flap. Light flurries had begun, but this was common on the Col. There was no sign of severe weather.

"We're fine up here," Cicero reported. "And you should be, too. If that squall was anything to worry about, the forecasting services would have given us a heads-up."

Perry looked around the cramped space. "Where's the sat phone?"

The team leader finally found it in the other tent, beside Sammi's slumbering form. It was still hooked into Tilt's computer. The second he pulled out the jack, the phone began to ring.

Cicero picked up the handset. "This is Cap."

It was the American forecasting service. They had been calling for hours. A major storm had formed unexpectedly, rising from the Khumbu valley right up to Mount Everest.

EVEREST

"So batten down the hatches," the meteorologist advised. "It'll be over by morning, but it's going to be a real interesting night. Your people are all off the mountain, right?"

"Of course," Cicero replied. Then it hit him. Where was Tilt?

Sammi stirred. Sleep was elusive, even for the weary, at twenty-six thousand feet. "What's going on, Cap?"

"Have you seen Crowley?"

"He's probably learning German so he can brag in every camp on the Col." She sat up. "He can't be far. His computer's still on."

"Don't you kids ever shut anything off?" Cicero asked irritably. Electricity was precious on the mountain, where the extreme cold drained batteries four times faster than normal. He opened the screen and reached for the power switch.

The E-mail recipient's address jumped out at him: **bv@national-daily.com.**

The *National Daily*!

Rage filled him. It was *Tilt* leaking information about SummitQuest to the *National Daily*! Tilt always screamed the loudest whenever Sammi tried to blame it on Ethan Zaph. And it was Crowley all along!

I should have known! Cicero ranted inwardly. Who else would do something this lousy? And keep on doing it when he saw how much trouble he was causing. Thanks to Tilt and the *National Daily*, poor Dominic was sitting at Base Camp, heartbroken!

The part that really burned Cicero was that Crowley was now the star of SummitQuest. They were all going to be expected to smile and pat him on the back while telling reporters what a great kid he was.

Instead of throttling the no-good . . .

Then he read the E-mail.

"Dominic?"

"Yeah, he really missed out," Sammi said wanly. "I wish I'd made it to the top, but I'd feel worse stuck on the sidelines."

Cicero bounded out of the tent, pulled aside his oxygen mask, and began to bellow, *"Crowley! Crowley!"*

Sammi was mystified. Of all people, Cap Cicero knew that no voice would carry very far through the screaming winds of Camp Four.

That was when she realized something she had not noticed before. She poked her head out the flap. "Cap!" she called up at him. "Tilt's wind suit! It's gone!"

Impossible, thought Cicero. There was no way the kid could have the strength to climb. Besides, where would he go? He had already made the summit.

He grabbed a walkie-talkie, feeling foolish. "Crowley," he mumbled. Then, louder, "Can you hear me, Crowley? Are you there?"

He was just about to put the handset away when Tilt's tired voice replied, "Hi, Cap."

"Where are you?" barked Cicero. "Why aren't you in camp?"

"The shrimp is out here somewhere," Tilt explained breathlessly. "He shadowed us up the mountain with This Way Up. With Zaph."

Cicero struggled for calm. "If they're climbing, they'll be coming back soon — "

"They should have been down hours ago!" Tilt interrupted. "They had oxygen trouble at twenty-eight thousand!"

"Oxygen trouble?" Suspicion edged into the team leader's voice. "And you know this because . . ."

Muffled sobs carried from the other end of the connection. "I didn't mean to hurt anybody! I was just trying to keep him off the summit! I wanted to be the youngest — I *need* to be the youngest — "

"*What did you do?*"

"I cranked his gas up to full." Tilt was weeping openly now. "Just to turn him around before the top! But something must have gone wrong!"

Of course something went wrong! Cicero wanted to howl. *Climbing Everest is hard enough when everything goes right!*

Money — that was the cause of all this. Oh, how Cicero yearned for the old days! Before the endorsements and the magazine covers and big companies like Summit that were willing to pour millions into no-holds-barred assaults on the great peaks. Back then, alpinists were dirt-poor fanatics who lived on macaroni and cheese until they could sign on with an expedition. Booby-trapping a teammate's oxygen was unheard of, because it didn't matter who was youngest or fastest or first. Records were for bragging rights, period. Yes, Tilt had done something terrible. But the real culprit was the cash and glitz that could turn athletes into terrorists.

With much effort, he swallowed his rage. Wherever Dominic was right now, it wasn't going to help the kid if Tilt got himself killed. "Listen, Crowley," he said through clenched teeth. "No one is blaming you. The stakes are as high as the altitude, and people do crazy things. But you've got to come back to camp. There's a storm brewing — a bad one. If you get caught out there, I can't help you."

Tilt was aghast. "The shrimp!" he cried, and the connection was broken.

"Crowley!" Cicero exclaimed, but there was no one on the other end.

Cap Cicero was renowned for coolness under fire, but right now he was anything but cool. Part of him was aware that he wasn't making much sense as he babbled a short explanation through the flap of the guides' shelter. "Talk that idiot down! Lie to him! Whatever he wants to hear! Just get him back!"

The snow was growing in intensity as he bounded across the Col to Angus Harris's tent in the This Way Up camp.

Harris was in his bedroll, just drifting off to sleep after eighteen hours on the mountain, when Cicero barged in.

"You let my kid climb without telling me?" Before the semiconscious Harris could manufacture a single word of reply, Cicero grabbed the other team leader's walkie-talkie. "Zaph, this is Cap Cicero! Can you hear me?"

"Let me explain — " Harris began groggily.

But right then Ethan's excited voice crackled from the handset.

"Cap, we're on the summit!"

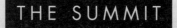

THE SUMMIT

CHAPTER SEVENTEEN

It had taken Ethan and Dominic more than four hours to ascend the summit ridge — double the usual time. One of them was always climbing in oxygenless slow motion. They passed the breathing apparatus back and forth, eating up valuable minutes.

At the Hillary Step, Ethan had tried to lower the rig to his companion. The cylinder slipped out of the loop, dropped forty feet, and disappeared into deep powder. In his fevered state, Dominic could not seem to locate it. Far above, Ethan pointed and screamed while the younger boy dug through the snow. By the time he had retrieved the bottle and jumared up the Step, another precious hour had passed.

But the summit! Dominic had seen well over a thousand photographs of the famous pinnacle. All of them, blown up to life size and arranged in a 360-degree panorama, could not begin to compare with the experience of being there.

He would not even permit himself to blink, for fear of missing a nanosecond of this ultimate experience. He and Ethan hugged and laughed like madmen, trading breaths from their single mask. The full wrath of the jet stream battered them, packing the punch of a spectacular windchill. Dominic barely noticed. The many stumbling blocks that had littered his path on this unlikely ascent fell away like the vast expanse laid out before him in every direction. Too young and too small — maybe so. But Dominic Alexis was on top of the world.

Ethan reached inside his wind-suit collar and pulled the vial of Dead Sea sand over his head. "I think this belongs to you."

Dominic stared at the necklace. In his exhausted elation, he had completely forgotten Chris's memento from the lowest point on the globe. It was hard to believe that its long journey was finally over. It had traveled up so many crags, so many cliffs, so many mountains. And here, seven miles above its starting point, the keepsake had risen the full range of altitude the planet had to offer.

We did it, Chris. If only you could be here to see this with me.

Dominic's voice was hoarse as he spoke his brother's often-repeated words to the small vial: "Far from home, baby. You're far from home."

That was when the call had come over Ethan's walkie-talkie.

"Shhh!" Dominic hissed. "Don't tell Cap I'm with you!"

"Do you think I'm deaf?" the tinny voice from the small speaker raged. "Let me talk to my climber!"

Dominic leaned over to the handset and bellowed, "No, Cap! You don't know I'm here!"

"Forget about that!" came the impatient reply. "Don't you see you're in trouble? *Nobody* summits this late! Neither of you is going to be anywhere if you don't get down from there!"

"We read you," agreed Ethan, much deflated. "We've had some delays — oxygen problems. We're descending."

"Not so fast," snapped Cicero. "There's a blizzard coming on the south side — a monster. It's already snowing at the Col. You can't beat it."

Dominic turned around. Angry dark clouds smothered the Khumbu glacier all the way into the valley, engulfing everything but the peak of Lhotse. On Everest, the storm was creeping up to the Balcony and the southeast ridge. They were trapped! "But — " he stammered, "but we can't just stay on the summit — "

"There's a British team on the North Face," Cicero told them. "They left a camp at twenty-seven thousand. That's a thousand feet closer, plus the mountain will block the storm for a while."

The North Face! Most Everest ascents followed the southern approach, but there were other, even more difficult, routes to the top.

"I don't know, Cap," Ethan said nervously. "It'll be dark soon, and neither of us has ever been on the north side."

"I'll talk you through it," Cicero promised. "You'll have to rappel down two big cliffs, but at least you'll be going down, not up."

Dominic hesitated. "Are you sure there isn't another way?" He had faith that his body would not let him down. It was his mind he didn't trust. In his oxygen-depleted state, did he have the powers of reason to learn a notoriously difficult new route in the dark, with a killer storm bearing down?

"Listen, kid," Cicero said patiently. "Things happen in mountaineering. A few dumb decisions, a little bad luck; before you know it, you're in a jam. You can survive this — but not on the southeast ridge."

Dominic's eyes met Ethan's. Cicero had climbed the North Face before. If anyone could guide them, he could.

Dominic knelt down and set Chris's necklace

in the firm snow beside the Summit Athletic flag Tilt and Sneezy had planted many hours earlier. He regarded it oddly. "No," he said suddenly, vehemently. This thing had meant good luck for him every step of the way. It had even led him to the winning entry in the contest that had qualified him for SummitQuest's boot camp.

Sorry, Chris, but I need it more than any mountain does!

Carefully, he picked up the glass bottle, unscrewed it, and let a few grains of Dead Sea sand fall to the pinnacle of the world. Then he closed the vial and strung the leather strap over his head. "Let's move."

At six fifty-five P.M., Ethan Zaph and Dominic Alexis stepped into the unknown on the North Face of Everest. As they left the summit, they entered another country. The ridge marked the border between Nepal and Tibet.

They had only been descending for twenty minutes when Cicero's voice on the walkie-talkie began to grow more faint amid the crackling static.

Ethan was alarmed. "Cap! We're losing you! The mountain's blocking the signal!"

"It doesn't work that way, kid," Cicero soothed.

But as they continued to negotiate the rocks,

the team leader faded into the howl of the jet stream.

"You're gone! You're totally gone!" Ethan shouted into the handset. "Cap! Can you read me?" He shook the unit violently. "This isn't supposed to happen! I can't even hear the static anymore!"

Dominic's mind wrestled with the altitude. "Dead batteries?"

"We've got no spares!" Ethan held the handset close enough to swallow it. *"Cap! We need you! You can't leave us!"*

But the walkie-talkie was silent. They were on their own on the treacherous North Face. Dominic felt the absence of Cicero's voice as sharply as if the team leader had been climbing right beside them.

He passed Ethan the oxygen mask, and the older boy gratefully took a gasping suck.

To their left, the peak of Cho Oyu, the sixth highest mountain on Earth, fell into darkness as the sun dipped farther beneath the horizon. Soon it would be Everest's turn.

Several hundred feet below them, the sullen gray clouds of the storm began to wrap around the base of the summit pyramid.

THE SUMMIT

CHAPTER EIGHTEEN

"Kid? Zaph?" In a rage, Cicero bounced the walkie-talkie off the wall of Angus Harris's small shelter.

"What?" the This Way Up team leader asked anxiously.

"Keep trying to reach them!" Cicero tossed over his shoulder as he scrambled through the flap. "I've got another missing kid to check on!"

Outside, the blizzard was revving up to its full fury. The rocks of the Col were already covered with three inches of fresh snow.

He could barely squeeze himself into the jam-packed SummitQuest guides' tent. Sammi had joined the vigil around the radio. Dr. Oberman hunched over the set, pleading with Tilt.

"Climbing is *suicide* in this weather!" she shrilled. "You summited; you're a star! Don't throw your life away just when you've got everything you always wanted!"

"I want the shrimp," Tilt panted in reply. "And Zaph. I'm not coming down without them."

Sammi grabbed the microphone from the doctor's hand. "Tilt, it's Sammi. Listen, Dominic and Ethan are safe on the Col."

"You're lying."

"They're at the Germans' camp," Sammi insisted. "Hanging with some of their Sherpas. You know Dominic and the Sherpas."

It brought a rueful laugh over the speaker. "Nice try."

Cicero considered giving Tilt the news that Ethan and Dominic had already summited and were currently descending the North Face, far out of anyone's reach.

No, he thought. *The kid's consumed with guilt. He might try to climb the mountain again and chase them down the other side.*

He hefted the microphone. "Crowley, if you don't get your butt down to Camp Four, I'm coming up after you."

"It's about time," Tilt shot back. "But don't worry about me. Find the shrimp."

And he broke the connection.

Nearly flattening Sneezy with a knee, Cicero began to pull on his wind suit. Babu reached for his own gear.

"This isn't smart," Dr. Oberman said seriously. "You guys are as good as it gets, but in these conditions, the mountain always has the upper hand."

Cicero could only shrug helplessly as he continued to dress. That had been the problem with SummitQuest from the beginning. The rules and procedures on Everest had been established for decades. But it was always assumed that the alpinists were *adults*. Certainly, if Tilt were twenty-four and not fourteen, no rescue party would be sent until after the storm. A ninth grader was a whole new ballgame.

Outside, they strapped on crampons and plucked helmet lamps from the equipment dump between the two tents. Babu switched his on. The sudden light only underscored the horrible weather. Driving snow blew horizontally across the Col. Visibility was practically zero.

Babu hesitated a moment. Then he selected an oxygen rig from the pile and shrugged into it, fitting the unfamiliar mask over his mouth and nose.

Cicero watched him soberly. In all the decades the two men had climbed together, Babu Pemba had never once breathed bottled gas, not even at the summit. That he felt the need to do so now was as urgent a warning as any forecasting service could ever give.

It was going to be a long night.

It turned out to be Ethan who drew the last lungful of bottled O's from their single cylinder. Dominic recognized the little choking gurgle that came from his companion.

"Empty?" he asked.

"Done." Panting, Ethan shrugged out of the apparatus and let it drop to the rocks.

It was not their first piece of bad news. As night finally enveloped the top of the world, they had switched on their helmet lamps to discover that only Dominic's was still working. One less asset. One less lifeline.

And the storm. It had begun slowly, but soon made up for lost time. The gale drove snow into their faces, standing them erect as they struggled to hunch forward. Powder covered the rocks almost immediately, making the route slippery and even more dangerous.

"What happened to Cap's cliffs?" Ethan shouted over the wind.

Dominic cleared the snow from his watch. They were just above twenty-eight thousand feet. He had read about the famous Steps of the north side. He wrestled with his hazy memory, trying to think back — trying to think *period!* The uppermost of the two cliffs — surely they should have reached it by now. . . .

"But how could we have missed it?" he asked.

"We veered east!"

"Yeah?" In the blinding blizzard, Dominic had

no trouble believing it. But with a flutter of panic, he realized that it would have made just as much sense to him if Ethan had said they'd wandered to the west. "Are you sure?"

"I think so!" The older boy seemed less certain, confused.

They spun around desperately. The storm surrounded them like the curtain ringing an old-fashioned bathtub. Even with his helmet lamp, Dominic couldn't see much farther than a few feet through the squall. The more he looked, the more disoriented he became, until all directions seemed equally promising.

He was relieved when Ethan started off again. Dominic hurried ahead, leading the way with his torch.

The ground grew more jagged and unpredictable. For over an hour, they slowly descended. Dominic trained his helmet lamp downward, focusing on one footfall at a time. Ethan followed right behind, step-by-step in Dominic's tracks in the accumulating snow. It was the only safe course.

All at once, a blast of wind was followed by an instant of calm, creating a small gap in the blizzard's cloak. Dominic saw . . . *nothing!*

No rock. No ice. No slope, gentle or steep, unfolding ahead.

He got down on his hands and knees and crawled forward. *Stupid,* he scolded himself. *It was probably a hallucination.*

And then the beam of his helmet lamp shone on snow-covered ground — *sixty feet straight down.*

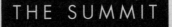

CHAPTER NINETEEN

The cliff! They weren't lost after all!

The celebration was short-lived. Ethan and Dominic peered over the lip and examined the obstacle below. The step was formed by the crumbly mustard-colored rock of the Yellow Band. Ethan reached out and grabbed a handhold experimentally. It disintegrated in his hand.

"Doesn't matter," he said in answer to Dominic's apprehensive look. "We can't stay here."

Using the blunt end of his ice ax, Ethan pounded a piton into the top of the cliff. The rotten rock shattered around it. He tried several other places with similar results.

"Let me try." Dominic threaded a line through the peg's ring, and tightly wound it around a bulbous outcropping of limestone. Then he hammered the piton into a small crack beneath the boulder.

Ethan tested the cord, pulling with his full weight. Amazingly, it held. "I'll lead."

While Dominic shone his light on the route, Ethan attached his harness to the top rope and began to rappel carefully down. Whenever his crampons made contact with the brittle limestone of the cliff, he would dislodge a cascade of pebbles. Other than that, the descent was routine, and he was at the bottom in a matter of minutes.

"It's okay!" came the call from below.

Dominic clipped onto the line and heaved himself over the side.

The feeling of the rappel buoyed Dominic's spirit, dissipating the dread that gripped him. *This* was something he was good at, something he had control of. He stopped on a narrow, snow-covered ledge halfway down to catch his breath. But when he pushed off again, he was instantly aware that something was not right.

High above, a weak spot in the anchoring rock gave way under his weight. The outcropping broke in two, sending a large chunk of limestone tumbling over the lip of the cliff. He saw the boulder hurtling down at him for just a second before the piton popped out, and he was falling, too.

The warning formed in his mind: *Ethan, run!* In the blinding blizzard, his companion would not see him until it was too late. But the drop took away what little breath he had left.

Ethan cried out in shock as the younger boy landed on top of him. Dominic felt his ankle twist — a sharp, searing pain shot up his leg. The visible world lurched violently as his helmet lamp was jarred off his head. There was a sickening pop as the plummeting rock shattered the torch as if it had been aimed by an evil spirit.

The North Face went dark.

"Shrimp!!"

Tilt blundered around in the blizzard, his crampons plowing through nearly a foot of new powder to bite into the ice below. Last night, he had been charged with such high excitement that he had barely noticed a mountain beneath his feet. But now, Everest was making its presence felt. The steepness. The altitude. The weather. *Ugh!*

"Shrimp! Zaph!"

He knew that the chance that the two boys might hear his cries was outrageously slim. But what else could he do? It was his fault they were in trouble in the first place.

Keep moving. One foot in front of the other. No pain.

The howl of the gale abated for a moment, and Tilt could make out Cicero raving at him through the walkie-talkie. ". . . *this-is-no-joke-Crowley-the-mountain-doesn't-care-that-you're-only-fourteen-you've-got-to-descend* . . ." Briefly, a smile replaced the grimace of fatigue on Tilt's face. The team leader was begging again. Just a few minutes ago, it had been gruesome tales of frostbite. Before that, threats. The climbers at Camp Four were trying to talk him down, too. He found their pleas kind of entertaining.

It's about time I got some attention on this expedition!

"Whoa!"

The beam of his helmet lamp illuminated his boot, frozen in midstride, about to step off the edge of the Kangshung Face.

In a panic, he overbalanced backward, and tumbled to the snow. He slid a little, then jammed his ax into the ice. At last, he stopped, his heartbeat a drumroll.

Man, that was close!

He got up again, dusting the snow from his wind suit. Where was he? The ascent to the Balcony was a straight shot from the South Col. It came nowhere near the Kangshung Face.

I must have wandered off. Understandable in the blinding snow.

Carefully, he climbed a few yards and began to retrace his steps. His tracks were already half buried under a coating of new powder.

As he headed back to the main route, a feeling of powerlessness took hold in the pit of his stomach. Getting lost in the blizzard was that easy — a single wrong turn had brought him

THE SUMMIT

within inches of disaster. Zaph and the shrimp could be anywhere, scattered over hundreds of millions of square feet of snow-obscured mountain.

Was there really any chance of ever finding them?

CHAPTER TWENTY

In the smothering dark at the base of the cliff, Ethan and Dominic took stock of themselves.

Dominic's ankle was sprained, but he could still walk in the tight supporting boot. Ethan's situation was more serious. A crampon point from Dominic's flailing foot had made a deep gash in Ethan's thigh. The cut itself was not an immediate danger. At this altitude, blood was the consistency of molasses, so bleeding was extremely slow. The problem was the slit in Ethan's wind suit, and in his sweatpants and thermal underwear underneath it. An Everester climbs in a cocoon. Once that shell is breached, there is no protection from the arctic cold of the Death Zone.

The contents of Ethan's knapsack were transferred to Dominic's. The younger boy wrapped the empty pack around Ethan's wound and lashed it on tight. They set out again, both hobbling — baby steps down the world's highest mountain. In the pitch-black, progress was almost nonexistent. Three painful, limping hours brought them only to 27,600 feet — the height of the Balcony on the south side. To keep from wandering

THE SUMMIT

in the zero visibility, they committed themselves to a narrow rock trench. It was a screaming wind tunnel in the gale, but at least it led down. They prayed it was in the right direction. The gully was so thin that they bumped and scraped their sides and shoulders on jagged formations of rock.

Another hour passed. The luminescent dial of Dominic's watch hovered before him like a floating spirit in the inky night. The blowing snow glowed an eerie green before it.

They held a nervous conference.

"Where's the second cliff?" panted Ethan, sucking air. "We should be there already."

"We must be off course," Dominic gasped. "Which means we'll never find that camp. We're going to have to bivouac."

Bivouac! To hole up and spend a night outside on the mountain. It was the last resort of a desperate climber.

Ethan was horrified. "In this cold? We'll be dead in an hour! We've got to keep descending!"

Dominic didn't have the strength to argue. But it was becoming increasingly clear to him that descent would not be an option much longer. They had been on the go for a solid day. They were both limping, exhausted, half delirious. In the absolute blackness, how long would it be before one of them took a fatal fall?

The gully seemed to widen as they slogged along, or at least Dominic wasn't bumping into its sides anymore. Eventually, he felt his crampons crunching hard ice instead of snow-covered rock. His heart sank. This only proved that they were hopelessly lost. He could not recall reading about a glacier this high up on the north side.

He was never really sure if he saw the crevasse, because that would have been impossible in the dark. More likely, he noticed his companion starting to stumble. He grabbed Ethan around the midsection, but it was too late. Ethan fell forward into the chasm with Dominic clamped on behind him. At the last second, the older boy flailed desperately at the lip of ice. His ax struck something solid and he held on for dear life. There they hung — Dominic onto Ethan, Ethan to the edge.

Dominic wanted to reach for his own ax, but he didn't dare release his grip on the older boy. Ethan clung to the mountain's rind. They were stuck — stuck until he lost his purchase, and they plummeted to depths unknown.

And then Ethan felt a front point scraping against hard ice below. "I'm letting go."

"Are you crazy?" rasped Dominic. "No!"

"Hang on!"

Dominic closed his eyes and steeled himself for the end. The drop was about six inches. The pounding of his heart reverberated in his ears. The pit was only seven feet deep.

He looked daggers at Ethan. "Why didn't you tell me?"

Ethan managed a thin smile. "You didn't ask."

By the meager light of Dominic's watch, the two investigated their surroundings. The shallow crevasse widened on the left side of the opening. There they found a small cavelike area, enclosed by a roof of ice. The refuge was still desperately cold, but it was protected from the punishing wind.

"Bivouac?" asked Dominic.

"Right."

They sat down on the rime, huddled together for warmth. Both knew they were lucky to find shelter from the elements. They could not have lasted much longer against the storm. But a night outside in the notorious Death Zone was by no means a sure thing. They were bone weary, and had no oxygen to warm and sustain them.

"No sleeping," Ethan shivered. "Sleep here and you'll wake up dead."

"Gotcha." Teeth chattering, Dominic didn't say what both of them felt: *I'm not going to miss out on a second of what little time I have left.*

Tired.

The word had become Tilt's universe. He was too tired to climb. Too tired to descend. Too tired to talk. Too tired to breathe.

He sat in the fresh snow — where? He had no idea. Seven hours of wandering had brought him no closer to the depression that was the route between Camp Four and the Balcony. He was barely aware of his physical body, a being of pure fatigue.

Sitting — that was where the trouble had started. He had plunked down in a snowdrift abruptly when his oxygen had cut out. It was no big deal — ice buildup in the regulator tube. But as of this moment, he had not yet cleared it. And it was just beginning to come through to his muddled mind that he had been stalled there for a long time.

His walkie-talkie crackled to life — Babu, hailing Cicero. "Cap, I'm on the Balcony. No sign of him. No sign anybody's been here for a while."

"*Crowley!*" bellowed Cicero, and kept on yelling.

THE SUMMIT

Tilt had been ignoring the team leader's calls all night. But something told him the situation had changed.

Pressing the TALK button on the handset took all his concentration. "Hi, Cap."

"Kid, where the blazes are you?"

"I'm — I'm sitting down," Tilt mumbled.

"Get up!" Cicero almost screamed. "Climb up, down, sideways — just *move*!"

"Funny thing," Tilt replied in an almost amused tone. "I *can't*."

"You have to!" Cicero begged. "That's hypothermia talking! Climbing's the only way to fight it off!"

"I feel pretty warm," Tilt said in slight surprise. And he did. The bone-cracking chill of a few minutes ago seemed to have let up. His hands and feet felt numb rather than cold. Numbness of the extremities — that was important somehow. A serious problem. But he couldn't for the life of him remember why. Nor did he remember the first rule of the Himalayas — that Everest's deadliest weapon was not a crevasse or an avalanche or a collapsing serac. It was what was happening at this very moment: An exhausted alpinist, every milligram of energy wrung from his soul by a monstrous and indifferent mountain, simply ceases to fight.

Cicero was still yelling, but the voice seemed distant now. Had Tilt looked down, he would have noticed that the walkie-talkie had slipped from his mitt to the snow.

The weather was still unbelievably bad. Tilt wasn't worried for himself. He was a powerful climber with incredible stamina — the youngest ever to summit this pile of rocks. But the shrimp probably wasn't going to make it. On the way to the summit, Tilt had passed bodies, frozen solid, far too high ever to be recovered. The poor little kid would be one of those — the smallest.

But Tilt was strong. He had to be to feel comfortable in conditions like these. Odd — the warmer he felt, the less he seemed able to move his arms and legs.

Maybe all he needed was a short bivouac — a power nap. It might not be too late for the shrimp after all. When Tilt was fresh and rested, he would climb up and find Dominic. Wouldn't that be something — the youngest summiteer in Everest history coming down off the mountain with a lost boy under his arm? An impossible rescue!

As Tilt drifted off into the sleep from which he would never awaken, he was in the bright lights of that press conference. A jumble of microphones sat on the table in front of him. Reporters hung on every word to come out of the mouth of the great hero of Everest. His mother glowed with pride. The nobody from Cincinnati had traveled far and climbed high and finally reached his dream. Tilt Crowley would not be delivering papers anymore.

Flashbulbs went off until all he could see were spreading blobs of color, disappearing into a background of black.

CHAPTER TWENTY-ONE

The next thing Dominic felt was a sharp pain in the center of his forehead. It was a familiar sensation. Almost like . . .

Brain freeze! From gobbling too much ice cream too fast. Only — the growling of his stomach told him that he hadn't eaten ice cream — or anything else — for a long time. Where was he?

He sprang up with a jolt, banging his head on the ice roof of the crevasse. A cloud of fresh snow flaked off him. No wonder he had brain freeze. He'd been breathing the stuff in all night! A half-inch layer of powder had settled over him from head to toe while he was asleep —

"*Asleep?*" he cried in horror. "*No!*" Sunlight streamed in through the chasm's opening. It was morning! He checked his watch: five thirty-three A.M. They had spent an entire night outside at nearly twenty-seven thousand feet!

Ethan came awake, shaking off his own frosty coating. "What?"

Dominic wiggled his fingers and toes. "I can feel everything! You?"

The older boy did an inventory of his extremities. "No frostbite. This crevasse saved our necks!"

Dominic tried to exhale and found himself puffing on the thin air. "We are so lucky!"

"Not yet," Ethan said gravely. He checked his pack, still lashed around the wound on his thigh. "I feel pretty good, but that's only compared with how I felt last night. I'll bet we're too weak to realize how weak we are."

Just *how* weak became clear when they tried to get out of the crevasse. Two alpinists who had reached the top of the world yesterday were unable to extricate themselves from a seven-foot hole. Finally, Dominic worked his way to the surface by means of his front points and two ice axes. He helped Ethan up after him. Elapsed time: thirty minutes. It should have been thirty seconds.

As for where they were, that was another mystery. While the upper mountain was in bright sunlight, a layer of mist hung below them at about twenty-five thousand feet. The summit of Cho Oyu, poking up through the fog, confirmed that they were on the Tibetan side of Everest. But more than that they could not tell. Their crevasse was in a hollow in the mountain's flank, so their view of the great North Face was blocked.

"But if this is the north, what happened to the second cliff?" Dominic asked.

Ethan shrugged. "We must have worked around it somehow. Who knows where we were going in that crazy storm? Just be happy we can see again."

As it turned out, sight was of little value to two climbers who barely had the strength to walk. They had only descended a hundred feet when they found themselves in a steep rock depression, plowing through thigh-deep powder. Each step was a wrestling match — a war against snow, against fatigue, against breathlessness, against pain. *Pain — there's plenty of that.* Dominic's sprained ankle stiffened with every movement.

The ditch seemed endless, cutting diagonally to their left before disappearing into the mist a thousand feet below. The morning disappeared with it, hour by hour, swallowed up by this interminable descent from light into fog.

Struggling a few yards ahead, the figure of Ethan suddenly blurred as Dominic began to sob. The feeling of hopelessness that came over him was so all-consuming that he was left completely hollow. He was less than an empty shell; he was *nothing* — the faintest wisp of life force propelling two robotic legs through deep snow.

"Hey, Dominic!" Ethan was pointing.

But Dominic had retreated inside himself. At

that moment, he was only the sound of his foot-steps. Crunch . . . crunch . . .

"Dominic, look!"

And there it was, appearing out of the haze like a ghostly, jagged highway — a great rocky ridge.

"It must be the north ridge!" cried Ethan.

But to Dominic it was much, much more.

It was hope.

Perry awoke to two kinds of ache. Broken ribs and . . .

Tilt.

This time he didn't cry. There had been plenty of tears last night — from climbers and guides alike. They had all heard the whole terrifying process over the radio: the comfortable warmth, the lethargy, the sense of well-being — right up to the moment when Tilt had spoken no more. According to Dr. Oberman, death would have come within hours in the unimaginable cold.

Perry's sorrow was made anxious, edgy as his thoughts turned to Dominic, somewhere on the north side with Ethan Zaph. Two teenagers, lost on unfamiliar ground, far beyond the rescue range of anyone on the Col.

But Tilt! If anybody was bulletproof, I would have guessed him.

In the months Perry had known the boy, he had experienced many emotions toward him — rage, hurt, envy, even admiration. Mourning — that had caught him off guard. Tilt was the best of them. The biggest, the strongest, the most determined. And yet, Perry was going home, while Tilt would remain on the mountain.

Cicero and Babu had searched until four o'clock in the morning. The team leader would have been out there still if Babu hadn't physically dragged him back to Camp Four. Perry was still haunted by their heated conversation, inadvertently broadcast to the Col by a walkie-talkie frozen in speak mode:

"Killing yourself won't bring Tilt back!" Babu had shouted. "People die here, Cap! You know that better than anybody!"

"Fourteen-year-old kids don't!" came the exhausted reply.

"Only because nobody ever brought them before!"

It had seemed heartless last night. Now Perry understood that Babu had been merely stating a fact. If kids were going to attempt Everest, it stood to reason that sooner or later one of them would perish on the mountain.

It turned out to be sooner rather than later. It turned out to be Tilt Crowley.

I never even said good-bye.

But of course, no alpinist ever knew in advance when he or she would be saying a final farewell to a teammate.

Perry thought of his school chess club back home. He had always enjoyed the game for its mental challenge. Now he appreciated its *predictability* more than anything else. Chess was governed by a set of rules that applied to all players. But to tackle Everest was to take on an opponent with a pocket full of extra queens that could appear anywhere on the board at a moment's notice. Poor Tilt had suddenly found himself surrounded by an overwhelming show of Everest's hidden firepower. He was checkmated before he knew what hit him.

Cicero and Babu slept for just ninety minutes. Babu set out to organize a team to look for Tilt's body. Every Sherpa on the Col volunteered to help, even Pasang, who had just recovered from snow blindness.

Cicero would be unavailable for the search party. In yet another cruel twist of fate, the forecasting services had officially called the start of the summer monsoon. Last night's storm was just the beginning, they said. It was time to get off the mountain. So the expedition leader's first responsibility became guiding Sammi and Perry down to Base Camp.

"Which happens right now," Cicero said firmly. "The weather only gets worse from here on in."

"But we can't — " Perry left the rest of his protest unsaid. No one had particularly liked Tilt Crowley. But leaving the Col felt like abandoning their teammate.

Cicero blew his stack. "Since when is this expedition a democracy? *I* decide when you climb! *I* decide when you don't! *I* decide when you eat, sleep, and go to the bathroom! And right now I decide that you *shut up!*"

The SummitQuest climbers and guides regarded him uneasily. Ever since Tilt's death, their leader had been as volatile as nitro. He had just gotten off the radio with the British North Face expedition. Four Sherpas were now on their way to the high camp to bring down Ethan and Dominic — *if* the lost summit party had even made it.

The strain seemed to be getting to Cap Cicero. Would the legendary alpinist be brought down by the very mountain that had made him famous?

Descent. The SummitQuest team's climb was far from over. The wind had died down, but it was foggy and bitter cold. Slogging through this freezer of misery, they would be tackling several of Everest's most celebrated nightmares — the Geneva Spur, the Yellow Band, and below that, the mile-high sloped ice of the Lhotse Face.

They were approaching Camp Three, hanging off the rope like a frost-nipped procession of clothespins, when the grim word came over Cicero's walkie-talkie. Babu, Pasang, and two other Sherpas had located Tilt's body. Their teammate had died only a few hundred yards from the rock gully that led back down to the Col. But in the zero visibility of last night's howling blizzard, he might as well have been on the moon.

He'd be better off on the moon, Perry thought bitterly. *At least then NASA could send a rocket to bring his body back to his family.*

At twenty-seven thousand feet, Tilt's remains could never be safely removed from the mountain. Even the most skilled Sherpas could not maneuver so much weight on a six-foot frame down two vertical miles of the toughest descent in the Himalayas. It was too much of a risk for the living to recover the dead. Babu and Pasang wrapped the frozen body in the fabric of a small tent they had salvaged from Camp Four. It was all the burial that Tilt Crowley would ever receive.

SummitQuest reached the upper Cwm around three o'clock, and the temperature jumped seventy degrees. Shedding clothing and stuffing snow under their hats, they staggered into ABC late in the afternoon. The British North Face expedition was already trying to radio them.

A team of four Sherpas had ascended to twenty-seven thousand feet to look for Ethan and Dominic. They found the high camp deserted. There was no sign that anyone had been there for at least a week.

CHAPTER TWENTY-TWO

The ridge was notched and craggy — an exhausting series of rock climbs. Cruel and unusual punishment for two teenagers already pushed beyond the limit of human endurance. Was some malevolent god reshaping Everest just to destroy them?

No conversation had passed between Ethan and Dominic since they had reached the ridge. It wasn't that they had nothing to say to each other. Dominic had been formulating the sentences for the past three hours: *I'm done. I have to stop. Tell Chris I got his sand to the top.* The image of his grieving family brought a sharp stabbing pain to a body that fatigue had dipped in Novocain. Picturing them — Mom, Dad, and Chris — drove his stumbling progress. *I can't quit. Not yet.* His gas tank was bone-dry. He had nothing more to give to this mountain.

Below them, a massive snow-covered shoulder was appearing out of the thinning mist. It had been a shock at first, but now he recognized it for what it really was — a death sentence. There was no North Shoulder of Everest. Which meant

EVEREST

this was not the north ridge. They were still lost — they had always been so. And lost they would remain. Forever.

Ethan was also bewildered by the titanic bulge in the mountain's bulk, but he lacked the strength to wrestle his confusion into the form of a question. Where were they? What was going on? What was this colossal buttress — itself the equal of all but the world's highest peaks?

The two boys continued to climb down. It made no sense; this was clearly the wrong path. But there was no thinking anymore, no logic. Only will — the will to keep moving.

Finally, they dropped to the shoulder, staggering together in an awkward embrace. It was not a celebration — they fell into each other for support, and found that neither had the power to offer any. After twelve hours of descent, this relatively flat ground seemed strange and disorienting.

Twenty-four thousand feet. They had left the summit a vertical mile above them. Yet Base Camp lay farther still in the opposite direction. They were nowhere — a place that was likely to be their tomb.

Reeling, Ethan and Dominic wobbled arm in arm across the shoulder and gazed through the mist over the valley below.

THE SUMMIT

EVEREST

It was . . . Dominic blinked —

It was . . . *no, impossible! It's a mirage — the final hallucination of a dying climber!*

The Western Cwm!

Ethan saw it, too. The expression on his famous face spoke volumes, but all he could manage aloud was a croaked "How?"

And Dominic had the answer. Oxygen-starved and close to shutdown, his fevered brain made the leap almost immediately. They had *never* been on the north ridge! Somehow in the storm, they had gotten themselves turned around and traversed to the *west* ridge — the most difficult, least traveled route up Everest! And now they were on the West Shoulder, a vertical half mile above the Cwm!

No wonder we never hit the second cliff. We were off the North Face!

He wanted to explain it to Ethan, to scream it all over the mountain. But there was so much to say, so much to do — and so little energy left. They were right above Camp Two, but the tents looked like Monopoly houses twenty-seven hundred feet below. It would be a challenging descent for a well-equipped climber on two days' rest. They were out of rope and out of strength.

At last, Dominic found the only words worth

wasting precious breath on. "We can do it," he barely whispered.

"We can do it." Ethan nodded.

They started down the rounded crest of the West Shoulder.

In all his years of climbing, Cap Cicero had never known such bottomless despair. Sure, he had lost teammates before — friends, even a couple of clients.

No kids. Never kids.

And now the mountain had devoured three teenagers, two of them under his care.

He didn't blame himself. Years of experience had taught him that. Everest chose when and where it would exact its toll, and from whom. The youth of these three victims had nothing to do with their fate. Ethan and Tilt had the size and strength of adults. And Dominic? He was small, but his smarts and stamina made him the toughest alpinist Cicero had ever seen.

I wish I could blame myself. Three kids are dead. Somebody should have to pay for it. Savagely, he drove his ax into the hard ice where he sat, feeling the temperature plunge minute by minute as the sun set on the Western Cwm.

His emotion went far beyond finger-pointing

and recrimination. He was staring at this mountain he knew so well as if he had never laid eyes on it before. *What are we doing here? What's the point of it all? What kind of people are we if we think it's worth this sacrifice to stand on the summit and take pictures with frozen fingers?*

"It doesn't make sense," he muttered aloud.

"Probably not," came a soft voice.

For the first time Cicero realized that Sammi was sitting beside him. She added, "But if it made sense to anybody, it would have been those three." She gave him a watery smile. "At least that's what I tell myself every time I think I'm going to lose it."

It's not enough, he said to himself. *At a certain point the price is just too high.* "Get some rest," he told her. "We've got the Icefall tomorrow."

"Okay." She stood up. "Cap? This Way Up, the Germans, and us — that's all there is on this side of the mountain, right?"

He looked at her. "So?"

"So who are those two guys up there?"

His eyes followed her pointing finger. There, halfway down the hulking West Shoulder, two tiny figures were descending. They looked like ants against a vast expanse of white.

Cicero wrenched the binoculars from his pack. The magnification brought the alpinists closer, but he could not make out faces. Yet he knew. A big guy and a little guy, their movements labored, their exhaustion plain. An extra-small red wind suit.

Unbelievable — no, that wasn't strong enough. *Miracle!* It was the *kid*, back from the dead! Dominic, and Zaph with him!

"*Andrea!*" he bellowed. "*Lenny!*"

And they were climbing, a blur of pure purpose. Cicero could not remember strapping on crampons, but there they were on his boots, biting into the ice and snow of the West Shoulder. Nor could he recall picking up rope. But an entire coil was slung over his shoulder. As he sprinted ahead of his guides, tears streamed down his cheeks. Cap Cicero had never wept at any tragedy on any mountain in a legendary thirty-one-year career. But the emotion of this moment welled up inside of him until a single body could not contain it anymore. Mighty Everest had given one back.

He could see their faces now — two young people, aged decades in forty-eight tumultuous hours. He shouted; they didn't. They *couldn't*. They were close to collapse.

THE SUMMIT

Cicero reached for Dominic's harness, and brought the boy to his embrace. Dr. Oberman and Sneezy flanked Ethan, each supporting an arm. The ordeal was over.

Camp Two waited below. Hot food, warm sleeping bags — life.

EPILOGUE

The memorial service was crowded. Tilt had come friendless to SummitQuest. He left the expedition much mourned by his teammates, the climbing world, and a nation that had read on the front pages of newspapers about his achievements and tragic death. The fourteen-year-old had reached his goal. Tilt Crowley was a household word.

There were more than a hundred people jammed into the small chapel, and that didn't include the horde of media camped in the parking lot outside. The SummitQuest team had been mobbed by reporters upon their arrival. Dominic, in particular, found himself besieged by cameras and microphones.

"Dominic, how does it feel to be the youngest human to stand on top of the world?"

"Do you think your new record has been overshadowed by Tilt's death?"

"Are you haunted by the fact that Tilt died trying to rescue you?"

Cap Cicero handled all questions for the team, and his message was short, if not sweet.

"Bug off!" And he slammed the door in the reporters' faces, shattering the long telephoto lens belonging to the photographer from the *National Daily*.

"Nice shot," whispered Sammi. "Hey, Cap, did you ever find out who was spying on us for those jerks?"

Cicero regarded his three surviving climbers. "No," he said evenly. "I guess we'll never know." Tilt Crowley had been no angel. But what was to be gained by speaking ill of the dead? The boy had paid for his crimes. And then some.

Dominic barely heard a word of the brief service. His mind still reeled from his introduction to Tilt's grief-stricken mother an hour before. The bereaved woman had looked at him with horrified loathing. He could tell that she held him responsible for her son's fate. Even now, seated in the second row of uncomfortable wooden chairs, he could feel her accusations filtering through the black lace kerchief that covered her hair.

A sympathetic hand patted Dominic's shoulder. Chris sat behind his younger brother, his shirt and tie concealing his vial of sand from the Dead Sea, now a few grains lighter. To his left were Ethan Zaph and Nestor Ali of This Way Up, and Bryn Fiedler, a former SummitQuest teammate. On the other side, Mr. Alexis, Sammi's parents, and Joe Sullivan himself paid their respects. As the sponsor of the ill-fated expedition, the billionaire CEO was also under fire from the media. But he had hardly left his nephew's side since Perry's return from Kathmandu.

The last of the speakers was Cap Cicero. He pointed to the life-size photograph of an exultant Tilt on the summit of Everest. "Look at that face and tell me Tilt Crowley was a victim. Not in a million years. He beat the mountain, not the other way around." He turned to the poster and flashed Tilt a thumbs-up, the alpinist's signal for success. "Congratulations, kid. You always told us you could do it."

An uncomfortable, almost hostile murmur rippled through the chapel. That was it? That was all this man had to say about the terrible death of a child entrusted to his care? What kind of callous monster was this so-called legend?

But the climbers in the room understood perfectly. Their backs straightened and their jaws set. Dominic could feel his right hand curling to the grip of an imaginary ice ax. Inside his stiff dress shoes, his feet formed to the contours of heavy mountaineering boots.

He was aware of a flicker deep inside that was half forgotten, yet instantly familiar. It had been extinguished during his descent of the West

Shoulder — at the awful moment when Cicero had told him the news about Tilt.

It was the urge to turn the axis of motion vertical. To defy gravity and leave the ground in search of some impossibly distant summit.

To *climb*.

GORDON KORMAN

started writing novels when he was about the same age as the characters in this book, with his first novel, *This Can't Be Happening at Macdonald Hall!*, published when he was fourteen. Since then, his novels have sold millions of copies around the world. Most recently, he is the author of *Swindle*, *Zoobreak*, and *Framed*, the trilogies Island, Everest, Dive, and Kidnapped, and the series On the Run. His other novels include *No More Dead Dogs* and *Son of the Mob*. He lives in New York with his family, and can be found on the web at **www.gordonkorman.com**.